RED RIVER
CROSSING

RED RIVER CROSSING

•

Kent Conwell

AVALON BOOKS
NEW YORK

© Copyright 2002 by Kent Conwell
Library of Congress Catalog Card Number: 2002090088
ISBN 0-8034-9540-4
All rights reserved.

Published by Thomas Bouregy & Co., Inc.
160 Madison Avenue, New York, NY 10016

PRINTED IN THE UNITED STATES OF AMERICA
ON ACID-FREE PAPER
BY HADDON CRAFTSMEN, BLOOMSBURG, PENNSYLVANIA

To my daughter, Amy.
Thanks for being you. I love you.

Chapter One

I survived being born near Injun Bayou on the Sabine River in the Piney Woods of East Texas in '48. I survived the War of Secession, what most Southerners called the Great War for Southern Independence. I survived a few months with that gallant Confederate heathen, Nathan Forrest Bedford, and I cried when General Lee gave his farewell to the Army of Northern Virginia.

Afterward, I survived a dozen gun battles with road agents, hide thieves, and rustlers, and I survived the Kiowa and Comanche under Chief Quanah Parker in the Texas Panhandle.

But none of those adventures prepared me for the trouble the crazy woman and her three daughters dumped in my lap at Red River Crossing.

Believe it or not, if I'd been given a choice between those females or squatting in a buffalo wallow and fighting off old Quanah Parker and his boys, I'd have taken the buffalo wallow every time.

But, life plays strange tricks on a body, and this was one of the strangest.

In the midst of a heavy rain, me and my sidekick, Buckskin Charlie Gowater, pulled up at the edge of the sandy riverbank that marked the north shore of the Red River. For the last two days, the clouds had dumped drenching rains over the countryside and lightning had raked the prairies. The broad river had risen, inundating the sage bushes along the bank.

Charlie, a Southern Ute from the Capote band, studied the river above us. "Flood come."

I squinted toward the far shore, but the heavy rain blocked it from view. The river could have been two hundred yards or even five hundred wide at this point.

Lightning cracked, charging the air with a tension that seemed to make your hair stand on end. We stood at a natural crossing. On either side of us, red sandstone bluffs rose twenty to thirty feet, pocked by caves.

Charlie indicated one. "Dry. Make fire. Wait for flood to go."

I shivered. I hated caves. There's a four-dollar word for the feeling I get when I enter one. I don't remember it, but I feel like I'm being all closed in.

The idea of a snug, dry refuge from the rainy weather was appealing, but we couldn't take the chance. For the last four days, we had ridden through Indian Territory where half-a-dozen Indian nations lived a restless existence. We hadn't spotted any skulking braves, but we both knew we were fools if we holed up here where a stray party could stumble across us.

I glanced at my saddlebags in which, along with a couple of my favorite books, reposed six thousand dollars in gold, three hundred double eagles, the result of two years hunting buffalo. As long as I had my saddlebags, I could handle any kind of weather. I pointed to the far bank.

Before I uttered a word, Charlie flashed a Devil-take-the-hindmost grin and bolted into the water. "We go," he shouted as a crack of lightning lit the darkening countryside with an ear-splitting crack.

Clenching my teeth, I slammed my heels into my roan's flanks. The wiry mustang leaped forward. I held my breath, my eyes on Charlie.

I'd crossed the Red several times. It was a river of quicksand. Club-footed ponies would sink, but the mustang, wiry and agile, could react instantly to the slightest change in the firmness of the riverbed.

The rain intensified. The river continued to rise, now halfway between the mustang's knee and shoulder.

I felt of the saddlebags. The unyielding bulk of the

gold coins and books brought a grin to my rain-streaked face despite the peril we were facing.

Suddenly, Charlie jerked his head around and squinted upriver. I followed his gaze, seeing nothing but the sheeting rain.

And then I heard it.

As he had predicted, the flood was coming.

I cursed my impatience. We should have found a cave. "Hey! Go, boy," I shouted, urging my pony forward, at the same time keeping my eyes on the thunderous sound racing toward me.

One moment I was peering at a heavy curtain of rain, and the next, at a wall of foam in the middle of which was a dark object. A log.

I grabbed at the saddlebags and tried to duck, but the flood slammed into me, and my head exploded.

Chapter Two

The next thing I remembered was the howl of the flood, like chained thunder, growling and throbbing. I clenched my teeth, awaiting the impact, except it never came. Only the roar.

Slowly, as I eased back into the world of the living, the roar shifted its tenor from the blur of a thunderous howl to the staccato beat of rain against a roof.

I opened an eye and stared at the shake roof over my head. The room was dark except for a flickering fire somewhere to my left. I turned my head and spotted a tiny flame in the hearth on the opposite wall. A dark figure covered with blankets lay on the floor between me and the fire.

For several moments, I lay motionless, staring into the darkness above me. I was alive, but that was all I

5

knew. And for the moment, all I cared about. I closed my eyes and slipped back into the comforting arms of sleep.

The rain still drummed against the roof when I next awakened. Light streamed through the windows, illuminating the room, which appeared more spacious than it had the night before.

A spider, a cast-iron pot with three short legs, dangled from the pot arm above a small fire. Steam sizzled from under the lid that had been placed askew on the spider. A coal oil lantern sat in the middle of the handhewn trestle table. An old woman sat at the table, her white hair frizzed out in every direction, carrying on an animated conversation with the lamp.

My left arm itched. I reached to scratch it only to discover it was bound tightly to my chest with my forearm snugged down to my belly. I struggled to move, and a wrenching pain sliced through my arm.

I groaned.

The old woman looked up. The surprise on her face faded into a smug expression that said I-told-you-so. She rose slowly and doddered over to me, shaking that full head of stringy white hair. "Now, Harry, you got to remain still. I told you last night. You can't go moving around with a busted arm. You hear me, Son?"

I looked up into her vacant eyes, my brain desperately trying to figure out just what in the Sam Hill was going on. Was I dead? Surely this couldn't be heaven with an old woman like this running loose. Was it the other place? Maybe so. After all, the good Lord knew I'd pulled enough stunts to deserve it.

A harsh voice cut through my confused thoughts. "Mother!"

I cut my eyes in the direction of the voice as a large-boned woman emerged from the doorway to the adjoining room. Wearing farmer's riggings, faded overalls, she appeared to be in her mid-thirties with her colorless hair pulled back severely and tied in a bun. She stomped toward us.

Her mother ignored her. The old lady just kept looking down at me. "Are you hungry, Harry? You didn't eat none last night, and Ruthie fried up your favorites, pork ribs and corn mush."

The younger woman bellowed again. "Ma! Go sit down and hush up." She came to stand by her ma and stare down at me. A white band of skin cut a swath across the top of her sun-tanned forehead. She eyed me coldly. "Well, well, well. Surprised you made it. Not that one less man would matter, but I figured you was a dead one." Her manner was as curt as her words were callous.

I nodded briefly. "Me too." I croaked.

She drew a deep breath and continued to study me, her lips twisted in a snarl. I had the distinct feeling that she was on the verge of sending me packing.

At that moment, a younger woman opened the door and paused when she spotted us. She uttered an exclamation of surprise and hurried across the room. "You're awake." She smiled down at me.

"Yes, ma'am," I mumbled, growing uncomfortable under three sets of female eyes despite the pain in my arm and the confusion milling about in my head.

Quickly, she retrieved a damp rag and bathed my face. "This will make you feel better, maybe good enough to try to eat."

"Much obliged, ma'am."

She had a pleasant though plain face, but her smile was enough to warm a body to the bone. "My name is Ruth," she said. "This is my ma, Mrs. Winkler, and my older sister, Deborah. We—"

Deborah interrupted. "You talk too much, Ruth."

Ruth kept her eyes on mine. "Don't pay her no attention. She's always been a bear."

Deborah tossed her head and turned back to the fire.

"Ma, why don't you get our patient some stew?" Ruth spoke to her Ma as she continued to bath my face.

I tried to shake my head, but the effort exhausted me. "I . . . I don't think I. . . ."

It was night when I awakened once again, this time ravenous as a starving wolf. A fourth woman had joined the three. Deborah and Ruth sat at the table, busy with paper and pencil. Old Mrs. Winkler rocked in front of the fire knitting while the other one sat on the hearth drying her hair. She looked to be the middle sister. I thought I spotted faint scars on her cheeks.

The ropes squeaked against the wood when I shifted in the bunk. All four sets of eyes turned to me. The older sister eyed me indifferently, the old lady vacantly, the middle sister, curiously, and Ruth, with concern.

Ruth hurried to my side. "How do you feel?"

"Hungry."

Ruth turned to the fire. "That's a good sign. This here is Sarah." She nodded to the fourth woman while spooning up a bowl of stew. "How's the arm?"

"Hurts. Is it broken?"

"Bad a break as I ever seen," Deborah said, resting her elbows on the table and leaning forward. "Bone broke the skin. I set it best I could."

"She used *alamo de hoja redonda* for the break," said Ruth. "You boil cottonwood bark to a thick liquid and spread it on. Helps the arm heal."

Sarah continued brushing her long black hair beside the fire. "Don't worry, cowboy. Deborah has set a passel of busted arms and legs. Once, she saved us an old mare by patching up her leg. Thought for a while we might have to shoot her, but she made it."

I grinned sheepishly. "Keep your six-guns holstered, ladies. I'm going to make it too." I glanced at Deborah, looking for a smile or at least some indication she appreciated my little joke. She shook her head and returned to her work.

Ruth tucked a pillow behind my head and offered a spoonful of stew. Eagerly, I sipped it. I stiffened. It was stew, but it had an odd taste, like bitter sage. I licked my lips and lied. "Good."

With a pleased smile, she continued feeding me. Despite the caustic taste, the stew was hot and filling. By the time I had two bowls down, I had grown accustomed to the taste and was ready for some answers.

Ruth must have recognized my curiosity for as I sipped on a cup of coffee thick enough to float a six-shooter, she brought me up to date.

"Sarah found you on the river bank after the river went down. We hauled you in here and did the best we could." She shrugged. "That was almost a week ago."

I frowned. "My partner, Buckskin Charlie. You find him anywhere? He's a Southern Ute," I added.

Deborah looked up. "If he lived through that flood, he'd better be mighty grateful I didn't find him."

That's when I got the hint Miss Deborah Winkler had a big hate for Indians.

"What about my horse, a roan mustang, and my saddle bags and my books?"

A look of disappointment furrowed Ruth's forehead. "Nothing like that. We brought you in just like you are."

I muttered a soft curse when I thought about my gold and my *Robinson Crusoe* and *Last of the Mohicans* books.

She continued. "Your six-gun was gone and the flood sucked your boots off, cowboy. All you had left was your clothes and that knife."

I spotted the stag handle of my knife protruding from my gunbelt on the wall. I nodded. "Much obliged. Name's Martin, Martin Wallace. Call me Marty."

She ignored my request. "Well, Mister Wallace, you are one lucky hombre. I'll tell you what I'll do. Tomorrow, I'll ride up and down the river and see what I can spot."

Ma Winkler, who had been absorbed in her knitting, looked around abruptly, her once vacant eyes animated with fear. "No. The Comanche and Kiowa wait out there. That's how I lost Steve." She looked at me, a puzzled frown knitting her forehead. "And Harry too, but he's back." She stared at me, her vacant eyes once again gleaming with animation for a fleeting moment. "I don't want to take a chance on losing any of you. Not again."

A fresh surge of pain rolled up my arm. I winced. "She's right. I'll be on my feet soon. If it's out there, it'll keep. I'll find it."

I saw a look of pain in Ruth's eyes. At the time, I couldn't figure it out.

Deborah snorted.

The next morning, the sound of bawling cattle awakened me. I lay motionless, letting my gaze play over my surroundings. The room was empty. The covered spider and a coffeepot sat in the coals on the hearth. A pair of worn brogans sat under my bunk. On a peg in the wall hung my gun belt, the holster empty. Without my boots and six-gun, I felt completely undressed. Except, I reminded myself, for my knife. I had a natural knack for the knife. Given my choice of only one of the two, I much preferred the knife over the handgun.

I moved to sit up, but the pain in my arm doubled me over. I clenched my teeth until the pain grew bearable. Barefoot, I gingerly made my way over to the door and peered out. Sweat beaded my forehead.

To my surprise, hundreds of steers were crossing the Red River downstream a short piece. Outside the barn, which was surrounded by cottonwoods, Deborah and Ruth were carrying on a conversation with a weathered cowpoke while two other cowboys were loading bags and boxes into a chuck wagon.

If I hadn't known better, I would have never guessed the two were sisters. One was rawboned, the other almost petite. Ruth was the size of her mother while Deborah stood a head taller.

"Why, good morning, Harry." Mrs. Winkler stopped at the corner of the cabin and beamed up at me. "Feeling better, son?"

About that time, Ruth spotted me. She spoke to Deborah, then hurried toward me.

Mrs. Winkler continued. "Come back inside and let

me get some mush, Harry. Ruth made it fresh this morning."

I remembered Ruth's stew. I cringed at the thought of her mush.

"You're up early," Ruth said brightly, stopping in front of us. She looked at her mother. "How's the garden, Ma?"

Ma Winkler nodded her head jerkily. "Good, child. I was going to get some corn mush for your brother."

Gently, the young woman turned her mother back toward the garden. "I'll do it, Ma. You take care of your corn and melons."

Inside, I slid in at the table while Ruth poured coffee. She studied me a moment, noting my drawn face and the sweat rolling down my cheeks. "Arm bad this morning?"

I tried to grin, but all I could do was chew on my lips and nod.

She reached into a parfleche bag hanging near the hearth and returned with a small clove, which she chopped into tiny pieces, scooped them into her hand, then offered them to me. "Here. Peyote. Wash it down with the coffee. It's better than laudanum."

Being familiar with the plant, I eagerly gulped it down as Ruth filled a bowl heaping full of corn mush and placed it in front of me. Being as hungry as I was, I would have eaten the bark off a tree. I hated corn mush having grown up on it back in East Texas.

"You'll have to overlook ma." She hesitated for a

moment as a shadow of guilt flickered across her face. "Both my brothers were killed by Indians. They killed Stephen first, then a few weeks later, Harry. When Harry died, something in her snapped. She . . . well, you see how she is." She poured herself a cup of coffee and sat across the table from me. For a moment, she gazed through me, drifting back into time, her face reflecting her pain.

I nodded in sympathy. "I understand."

The corn mush didn't have the taste of sage, but it was still corn mush. While I ate, she explained how they'd remained on the ranch raising a few head of cattle after her pa had died.

They supplemented their income by selling supplies to cattle herds pushing up the Chisholm Trail. Most of the supplies they purchased at Fort Sill, a couple days or so northwest.

"What about you? How'd you end up in the middle of the river?" She forced a grin.

I shrugged. "Long story. Truth is, I hightailed it out of the Texas Panhandle when all the Indian trouble started. As soon as the fight at Adobe Walls was over, Charlie and me lit a shuck for Injun Bayou on the Sabine River in the Piney Woods of East Texas." The mention of Buckskin Charlie's name brought on a fresh wave of remorse and regret.

"That where you're from?"

By now, the pain in my arm was subsiding. I tried to push aside the hurt I felt over losing a good friend.

"Yep. Sold enough buffalo skins to make enough money to buy my uncle's plantation back from the Yankee carpetbaggers. I was taking Buckskin Charlie with me. He's one of the Capote band of Southern Utes."

Before I could say another word, Sarah, her long, black hair streaming behind, burst into the cabin, squalling and boo-hooing like a seven-year-old child.

Chapter Three

I sat my coffee down with a start, splashing some across the top of the hand-hewn trestle table. Ruth leaped to her feet as her sister raced across the room and disappeared into the adjoining room.

"Sarah! What on earth—" She hurried after her sister.

Slowly, I hobbled to the door and peered into the bedroom.

Sarah lay sprawled face down on her bunk, crying just like someone had told her she was never going to have another birthday party.

Ruth was comforting her, but her words were too soft to hear. I stammered. "Can . . . can I do anything?"

"No," Ruth whispered softly over her shoulder.

I returned to the table and finished my coffee, wishing for a bag of Bull Durham. I glanced at my gun belt on the wall. No horse, no cigarettes, no hat, no boots, no six-gun. Blazes, I felt as naked as a newborn babe.

I slipped a hand in my pocket. At least, I had a few dollars.

Outside, the bawling of cattle fading into the distance told me the herd had crossed and was heading on north up the old Chisholm Trail.

A sudden weariness came over me. I stumbled back to my bunk and fell asleep.

I dreamed of Buckskin Charlie.

Strident voices awakened me. The words were vague and fuzzy, nonsensical in my head. I lay without moving, too weary to even open my eyes. Ruth's voice cut through the lassitude enveloping me. "Don't talk so loud. You'll wake him."

Deborah grunted. "I don't care. I ain't going to feed him for two weeks. He can make it on his own."

"He isn't going out there. He's too weak. I own just as much of this ranch as you do, and I say he's staying until he's fit and proper."

A trace of amused sarcasm edged the older sister's raspy voice. "What's wrong, little sister? You got your eyes set on that drifter?"

Ruth answered quickly. "Of course not. You know better than that. I got Ma to take care of. I can't think about nobody else," she added, her tone growing wistful. "Not now."

Deborah snorted. "Well then, little sister. Just don't you forget about him. We don't need no men around here. We've done just fine since Pa died . . . better, in fact, because now we got nobody to gamble away our money up at Fort Sill. All right, the cowpoke can stay, but only until he can travel."

Ruth's voice grew hard. She growled out the words between clenched teeth. "You aren't telling anybody how long they can stay, you hear me? If he needs to stay six months, he'll stay six months." Her tone challenged her sister.

For several seconds, a tense silence filled the room. Then Deborah stomped out the door.

I remained motionless, tussling with whether I should tell Ruth I overheard them or just remain silent. My arm decided for me.

A shard of pain brought an unbidden groan from my lips.

Ruth hurried to me. Concern filled her voice. "Mister Wallace. Are you all right?"

I heard her kneel beside my bunk. I opened my eyes. "Yeah, yeah. Just a twitch."

The lines on her forehead faded and she smiled. "I'll get your water and medicine."

The freshly drawn water was sweet and cold. I drank it greedily, savoring the relief it gave my parched lips and throat.

I sat up as she put the empty glass back on the table. "How's your sister?"

She looked at me curiously and glanced at the door through which Deborah had disappeared.

"Sarah," I added. "She feeling better?"

An expression of relief smoothed the lines on her face. She made a wry grin. With a note of pained tolerance, she explained. "Sarah is always wanting to fall in love. The Johannsons have a ranch about twenty miles west, and she had a crush on Wilaman, the Johannsons' boy. She learned yesterday that he had up and married Lucille Mae Shoop whose folks have a ranch back south."

"Oh. I'm sorry."

Ruth brushed her short brown hair from her eyes. Flippantly, she replied. "Don't be. Sarah falls in love at least twice a year."

Before I could reply, Deborah returned, ignoring me as she brought in an armload of firewood and dropped it on the hearth. I spoke to Ruth. "You wouldn't happen to have a pair of your brothers' or Pa's boots, would you? I get mighty uncomfortable just laying round. I'd like to pitch in to pay you back a little for all the trouble you gone too."

Ruth and Deborah exchanged a quick glance, but I didn't miss the smug look of triumph on Ruth's face. "Pa's won't fit," she said. "He was a small man. We buried Steve and Harry with theirs. I put an old pair of Deborah's brogans under your bunk. I reckon they might be some tight, but they should do you just fine. And I'll see if I can find an old Stetson around."

I was still weak, but I managed to haul in a few pieces of firewood, draw a bucket of water, and carry an armload of roasting ears Mrs. Winkler had picked into the cabin.

That night, I slept soundly.

The next few days, I made good progress, each day growing stronger, working more around the ranch, which was in fairly sad shape. The job was too much for two women. Sarah and Mrs. Winkler were no help, and running a ranch and maintaining a supply station for trail herds called for a heap more brawn and cussedness than Ruth and Deborah could muster.

I faced a dilemma. Soon I'd be well enough to ride. Should I thank them and ride out, or stay and give the ladies a hand with their problems? I'd been brought up to respect women, never to leave them in a bind. Besides, my gold was gone, so there was no way I could buy back what was left of Uncle Lige's plantation.

Looked like my decision had been made for me.

In the barn were several dried cowhides, a ready source of rawhide strips, indispensable on a ranch. At night by the fire, I managed to build me a set of moccasins, which were much more comfortable than Deborah's tight brogans.

Sarah looked up from drying her long hair. In the

firelight, the scars on her cheeks were more defined. "How did you learn to do that?"

I held up the almost completed moccasins in my hand. "Spent time with the Southern Ute." A wave of depression settled over me as I remembered how Buckskin Charlie Gowater taught me to make my own moccasins.

At the table, Deborah looked up from her books and snorted. "Blasted Injuns. Ain't none of them decent folk."

I studied her a moment. "Well, ma'am, you're right about a heap of them, but the Southern Ute, especially the Capote band, they're good people. I lived with them for a couple years after the war. That's where I met Buckskin Charlie. He was the one that got killed in the flood you folks pulled me from."

"I thought only the squaws made the moccasins," Sarah said.

Ruth paused in mending clothes and listened to our conversation. Mrs. Winkler just rocked back and forth, dividing her time between knitting and staring at the fire.

"That's right, but the braves learn it too. There's times they might have to build their own."

"They comfortable?"

I handed one to her. "See for yourself."

Though too large for her, she slipped it on and placed her foot on the floor. She nodded in appreciation. "Comfortable."

"It has three soles with a layer of grass between each one."

I handed the other one to Ruth. She nodded in surprise at its comfort.

"You ladies want me to make you a pair?"

Ruth and Sarah exchanged surprised looks, then both nodded and smiled broadly. "We'd love it," Ruth exclaimed.

"Good." I nodded enthusiastically. "I'll measure your feet and Mrs. Winkler's. How about you, Miss Deborah? You want me to make you a pair too?"

She shot me a baleful look. "I don't want nothing Injun touching my skin."

I kept a grin on my face though it was difficult. "Let me know if you change your mind."

"I won't."

That night, I studied the problems between Miss Deborah and me. Best I could figure, next to Indians, she hated men. I didn't want to aggravate her, and the only way I wouldn't was if I wasn't around.

But I was in a bind. I had no horse, no six-gun, plus the fact I owed these folks for taking me in. The only choice I saw was to stick it out. Help best I could around the place. Figure out a way to pick up some cash. Maybe I could hire on with the next herd, talk the trail boss into springing me for a horse and revolver, plus a few greenbacks for the Winklers.

Over the next few weeks, I made good progress. I

found four or five small jobs I could handle with one arm and without putting too much of a stress on my injury. And when I presented the ladies with their moccasins, they were thrilled.

One morning, I rose feeling pert and sassy. Ruth smiled, but I had the distinct feeling she was forcing it. "Looks like you feel better," she said, pouring the last of the water into the spider. She sat the bucket aside. "Coffee's ready. I'm mixing up a batch of corn mush."

"I'll get another bucket of water first," I replied, taking care not to reveal my dislike of corn mush. Even with honey or butter or jelly, mush clogged in my throat.

The few minutes outside gave me time to wonder about Miss Ruth. Seemed like the last few weeks as I grew better, she had become more distant, not really aloof, but not as warm and congenial as she had in the beginning. And for the life of me, I couldn't figure out what I had done to cause such a change in her.

The day was bright and fresh. Puffy white clouds drifted through a sky blue as a robin's egg. A few ponies stirred in the barn, and in the distance, cattle nibbled on the sparse graze. Dust puffed from under my feet as I walked.

As I cranked the bucket up, I heard a horse squeal from behind the barn followed by a shrill voice. Curious, I set the wooden bucket down and headed toward the commotion.

I jerked to a halt as I rounded the corner.

Deborah had a chestnut gelding snugged down to the snubbing post and was beating it across the head with a quirt, screaming obscenities at the animal.

"Hey!" I shouted, but she didn't hear me.

At that moment, I knew she must be a truly mean person. She hated Indians; she hated men; she hated horses; she hated me; and it appeared she hated even her family.

I stumbled through the corral rails and jerked the quirt from her hands. "That's enough," I yelled.

She spun on me, her eyes level with mine. She glared at me as if she wanted to kill me. She sputtered. "What—what—who do you think. . . ."

Before she could finish, I threw the quirt from the corral and stuck my nose in her face. "Look, lady, you don't ever beat an animal around me. Next time, I'll turn you over my knee." Since she probably outweighed me, I reckoned I would be hard put to pull off that job, but I was angry enough to bite off the ear of a lobo wolf.

"You can't come in here and. . . ."

I brushed past her to the chestnut. "I can and did."

"This is my place. I do what I want. I . . ." She was stammering and spitting as she babbled.

I fought to control the fury boiling my blood.

"Don't fret yourself, lady. I'm pulling out. I got no use for a body that beats on animals."

The chestnut ducked away, but I spoke gently. When my hand touched him, he seemed to relax. I'd always had a knack with animals, and this poor creature was no exception.

Behind me, Deborah cursed again, then stomped away.

The animal continued to gentle. I don't know what Deborah had in mind or what she wanted to do, but the gelding was a good animal, not real gentle, but not green broke.

After a few moments, I unsnapped his halter from the snubbing rope and continued talking and caressing him.

Ruth's voice came from behind. "You're leaving?"

I kept up my ministrations for the chestnut. "Yep. I been a boil on your sister's behind from the first. I'm much obliged to your folks for taking me in. Once I get settled in somewhere, I'll pay you for your trouble."

"It was no trouble, Mister Wallace. Just one of God's children helping another."

"Yes, ma'am."

"You don't have a horse or guns." Her concern seemed genuine.

"Figured I'd head south and hit up with a trail herd. Pour out my story to the trail boss and maybe he'll give me a knot-headed shavetail no one else wants."

"No. You can take that one there. And we have extra revolvers around. Old, but serviceable."

I looked at her, but she was staring at the chestnut. "Thanks."

"You're welcome."

I took a step back from the chestnut. For a moment, the animal stared at me, then stepped forward, ducking his head for my hand. I laughed and petted him. "Good boy. Now, you stay here."

I retrieved the bucket of water and headed back to the cabin. Ruth walked beside me. We were both silent. I was uncomfortable, and all I wanted to do was pull foot out of there as soon as I could. "I'd be obliged if you might make me loan of a handful of the peyote and a few biscuits. I. . . ."

We rounded the corner of the barn and jerked to a halt.

Ruth screamed.

Twenty feet in front of us sat a dozen Comanche warriors astride their war ponies.

Chapter Four

I froze, staring up into the leering faces streaked by war paint, at the same time cursing the naked spot on my hip where I once carried my six-gun.

They were a fierce looking band, each brawny warrior astride a muscular war pony. Naked from the waist up, their copper bodies glistened in the sun. Rock-hard fists clutched battered Winchesters and smoothly worn Osage orange bows. Their heavily muscled thighs gripped the ponies easily.

"Quiet," I muttered under my breath to Ruth. At the same time, my brain was frantically sorting and discarding my next move.

In that same instantaneous second, I wondered of the whereabouts of Deborah, desperately hoping she

27

wasn't standing in the shadows inside the house with her shotgun.

Then I recognized the leader.

I forced a crooked grin to my face and sat the water bucket on the ground. "Big Tree. It is good to see you. Much time has passed since I was in your camp." He was a Kiowa sub-chief, a violent, volatile warrior, difficult for Kicking Bird, the Kiowa chief, to control.

Quickly, I scanned the warriors behind him, spotting three more I knew, Black Coyote, Skywalker, and Sitting Bear, none of the three as I remembered given much to seeking peace.

Big Tree urged his pony forward a step. His black eyes narrowed as they took in my arm in a sling. "Wallace. Why you here? This place?" He swept the countryside with his eyes.

Ruth moved closer to me. "Easy," I muttered under my breath to her. I glanced at the open door into the cabin. All I saw were shadows. I dearly prayed that if Deborah was looking on that she would show more sense than she had in handling the chestnut pony in the corral.

I knew Indians well enough to know they were simply waiting for some indication of weakness before falling upon us. We were walking that proverbial top rail, waiting to see if we'd fall on one side or the other.

Skywalker and Sitting Bear eased their ponies up beside Big Tree. Skywalker leered down at me. We'd had our differences back at the Kiowa camp, but he was basically a coward.

With a sweep of my hand, I replied. "These my friends. I come far to help with the One-Who-Talks-to-Rocks."

The expression on Big Tree's face remained unreadable, but Skywalker and Sitting Bear couldn't hide the sudden alarm my announcement caused. Most tribes considered those souls touched in the head to be special, a product of their gods, and as such, to be shunned out of fear of being cast with an evil spell.

Big Tree studied the cabin a moment, and then rolled his axe-handle broad shoulders. "Where Wallace six-gun?"

I nodded to the cabin. "Inside. I have no need while I am with the One-Who-Talks-to-Rocks." I hoped my face wasn't revealing the near panic churning my belly. I indicated his warriors. "And now that my friend, Big Tree, and his braves have arrived, there is less for which me and my friends need to fear."

He studied me. Behind him, some of the warriors were mumbling to each other and looking around apprehensively. I decided to play my hole card. I whispered to Ruth. "Get your mother."

She looked up at me sharply. In surprise, she said. "What?"

Keeping my eyes on Big Tree and a grin on my face, I muttered. "You heard me. Your mother. Now."

Reluctantly, she disappeared into the cabin.

The warriors at the rear of the band moved forward, forming a single line facing me. I reckon I'd been in touchier predicaments, but to tell the truth, I couldn't think of any.

At that moment, a flash of sunlight from among the willow and sage across the river caught my eye. Was someone hiding in the willow brakes?

Clearing my throat, I frowned at Big Tree. "Why do the Kiowa leave the reservation? Is Kicking Bird still chief?"

Big Tree's fingers tightened about his Winchester until his knuckles turned white. "Kicking Bird is old woman. He fight no more." He held the Winchester against his massive chest. "Big Tree is now chief of the Kiowa."

I eyed the open door. Too far. Even if I made it, then what? I don't know if the Kiowa sub-chief caught my furtive glance or not, but he eased his pony forward, blocking my way.

At that moment, Mrs. Winkler, her stringy white hair standing on end like a broom, rushed from the house and halted immediately. She grabbed her apron with both hands and flapped it vigorously at the Kiowa as if she were shooing flies away from the table. "Shoosh! Out of here! All of you! Leave!"

The startled warriors yanked their ponies back a few steps. Two or three angry cries came from the rear, instantly ceasing when she hurried to me. She grabbed my arm. "Harry! Inside! I told you couldn't come out and play with your friends."

Worried mutters spread through the Kiowa band. They backed away quickly, eyes wide with fear.

I laid my hand on hers. "It's fine, Mrs. Winkler. This is Big Tree. He is a friend." Ruth stood in the door.

"But, Harry. They. . . ."

"Don't worry. Everything is fine." I patted her hand and gestured to the scowling Kiowa. "I want you to meet some of my old friends. This is *Addo-etta*, or Big Tree. Next to him is *Satank* or Sitting Bear, and this smiling one is *Mama-ti*, known to the white man as Skywalker."

Turning back to Big Tree, I indicated the water well. "There is water for your ponies, and you are welcome to share our food." At that moment, I was mighty grateful Ruth had tossed together a heap of corn mush.

I couldn't resist grinning when I thought just how lucky I would be if the Kiowa cleaned up all the corn mush in the spider. Then Ruth would cook something else for me. She was fine woman, but she had trouble with the frying pan.

From time to time as Big Tree and his warriors made short work of the corn mush, I glanced across the river in the direction from which the glint of sunlight had earlier emanated.

Glass? Maybe my gold? No, both sources were too

far-fetched. The only answer was a reflection off the barrel of a gun, a rifle probably.

While the Kiowa warriors devoured the mush, I stepped back inside the cabin.

Deborah stood beside the hearth, shotgun in hand. Sarah, her eyes wide with fear, cowered behind her while Mrs. Winkler rocked in her chair, knitting peacefully. I took my gun belt from the peg and glanced sidelong at Ruth. "You said you had a hand-gun?"

She nodded and quickly retrieved an old Navy Colt .36 Cap & Ball. It was ancient, but they had a supply of powder and balls and caps. Working with one hand was awkward, but I checked the action, and it was tight, so I quickly put in fresh loads, hefted the six-gun a few times, then dropped it in my holster, which I left just inside the door when I sauntered back out-side.

Ten minutes later, the Kiowa rode out.

Skywalker pulled up beside me and sneered. "I not forget you, Wallace."

Our eyes locked. I saw the hate in his. "I don't fight squaws," I said, spitting out the words.

He glared murderously, then jerked his pony around and raced after the others.

Ruth came to stand by my side. Deborah followed her out, shotgun in hand. She stopped behind us. To be honest, after our little set-to in the barn, I wasn't any too comfortable with her standing behind me with a loaded shotgun.

"Will they come back?" Ruth stood at my shoulder.

I tried unsuccessfully to forget Deborah. "Who knows? Maybe, maybe not. Big Tree will probably leave us alone. Skywalker? He could carve out my heart with a grin. There's trouble in the Indian nations. It could spill over down here." I glanced across the river again. Whoever had been over there was no greenhorn. A greenhorn would have shown himself, but this jasper remained hidden, except for the one time he had raised his rifle.

That had been when the dozen warriors had lined up facing me. I chewed on my lip. Was it possible? A slow grin cracked the frown on my face. If I were right—

I turned to Deborah. "If another Indian shows up, don't shoot." I laid my finger to my cheek. "He'll have a right ugly scar here."

She just stared at me, the fire in her eyes leaving no question about her feelings toward me.

Ruth sighed. "I was scared."

"You did good. So did your ma. She said just the right thing."

She grinned sheepishly. "I was scared."

I studied her a moment, sensing unspoken words on her part. "Just what did you tell her?"

She glanced at Deborah, then ducked her head. "Nothing. Not really."

"Well, you had to tell her something."

She shrugged. "Only that Harry was playing with his little friends, and they were fighting."

I stared at her a moment and then laughed. "It was the right thing."

Deborah snapped. "You should be ashamed of yourself, Ruth. Taking advantage of Ma like that. She can't help how she is."

"If she hadn't, Miss Deborah, we probably might all be dead about now." I went on to explain about the Indians and their superstitions toward those who appear touched. "Word spreads fast among the Indians. I doubt if you'll have trouble with them again."

Before she could reply, Mrs. Winkler's trembling voice called from inside. "Deborah! Ruth! Help!"

I jerked to a halt in the doorway. Sarah was on her knees, wailing and crying, dragging her fingernails down her cheeks, digging bloody gouges. Ruth and Deborah quickly pinned her arms as Mrs. Winkler tried to bathe the blood from her face.

Frowning, I remembered the faint scars on Sarah's cheeks and realized this incident had not been the first.

Sarah screamed and fought against them, trying to break free of their grasp, but Deborah and Ruth held fast.

"Can I help?" I took a step forward.

"Don't interfere." Deborah barked, shooting me a warning look.

After a few minutes of kicking and screaming, Sarah suddenly collapsed. Alarmed, I took a step in their direction, but Ruth shook her head as she and Deborah gently lifted their sister and carried her into the bedroom. "She's fine. She always faints at the end of one of her spells."

Mrs. Winkler tottered after them, water dripping from the washrag in her hand.

I stared into the bedroom, truly concerned. What kind of family had I fallen in with?

After a few moments, I went back outside and peered across the river. Maybe the reflection had not been from a rifle barrel. Perhaps it was simply the sun catching a dew-wet willow leaf.

Except, there had been no dew.

I waited expectantly all afternoon.

Nothing.

Sarah remained in the bedroom.

"We don't know what causes Sarah's spells," Ruth whispered softly as the logs crackled in the fireplace that evening. "She's had them for years."

Soon the fire grew low. I crawled into my bunk.

I don't mind admitting it, but I was restless that night. I didn't sleep but in bits and pieces. For more that one reason.

Had I allowed my imagination to run away with me earlier in the day when I spotted the reflection of sunlight? And second, were they all touched, the whole family? And third, if one sister had spells, what about the others? Deborah really worried me especially since she liked toting that shotgun. And just what kind of seizures would Ruth have?

Chapter Five

Rising well before the sun next morning, I stirred the banked fire and slid the coffeepot into the coals. I was feeling right spry. Within minutes, the others had risen, and Ruth was whipping up breakfast.

Even Sarah came out for breakfast, which naturally was corn mush. I've eaten corn mush every way possible, and I promise there is no spice, no dressing, no seasoning, no relish that will make it taste any better than corn-flavored cardboard confetti.

But I ate it. While I was choking it down, I made up my mind to catch us some fish. And instead of shelling and grinding all the corn into mush, why not boil some? Fresh roasting ears sounded mighty tasty. And a cook had to make a huge effort to ruin boiled corn.

At that moment a knock sounded at the door.

We looked at each other. Deborah pushed away from the table. "Trail herd due in. Probably the scout." She paused to grab her shotgun.

I turned back to my coffee, eying the bowl of mush on the table before me with some trepidation. But, it was filling, and I needed the energy.

Before I could take a bite, Deborah screamed. "Comanche!" In the next breath, the door slammed and the shotgun boomed twice.

Grabbing the .36 Navy Colt, I leaped back from the table. "Where?"

She pointed to the door that now had a couple two-inch holes in it. "Out there. I got him."

She stood facing the door, the shotgun trembling in her hands. I motioned her to the side of the door. "You best reload that greener."

"Huh? Oh. Yes, yes." Fumbling for the shells, she quickly reloaded. I nodded to the rope holding the locking bar in place and pointed outside. "When I give the word, yank the door open," I whispered. "Then slam it fast."

She reached for the rope. Gripping the .36 Navy Colt tightly, I whispered. "Now."

She jerked on the rope, and the door popped open. I stood staring at the bare ground. I muttered an oath. If she'd hit him, it wasn't hard.

In the next instant, the door slammed shut.

We stood pressed against the wall, staring at each other. "I'm going out. When—"

A deep voice came from outside. "Wallace!"

I frowned at Ruth. "Who in the blazes. . . ."

"Wallace. It's Charlie, Charlie Gowater. Tell that woman don't shoot."

Charlie? I grinned broadly. I yelled through the closed door. "Charlie? That really you?"

"Open up, Wallace. You don't, I'm heading out to Injun Bayou by my lonesome."

I relaxed. It was Charlie. "It's all right, Miss Deborah. You can lower that shotgun."

I threw open the door, and Buckskin Charlie stood staring somberly at me, his Sharps resting in the crook of his arm. I heard the click of hammers behind me. "No." I snapped at Deborah. "I told you, this is my friend, Charlie. Buckskin Charlie Gowater. The one I thought was dead. And he isn't no Comanche."

Deborah frowned. "He's still an Injun."

"Just be careful with that shotgun. He means you folks no harm."

I stepped outside and closed the door behind me. False dawn grayed the eastern sky. I grinned at Charlie. "When you said a flood was coming, you really meant a flood was coming."

He grunted and followed me a few feet from the cabin where we squatted on the hardpan. Charlie was thin and wiry like me. He wore a buckskin shirt, a loincloth, and knee-high moccasins. His long black hair fell over his shoulders.

I rested my elbows on my knees. "How did you find me?"

He made a sweeping gesture downriver with his hand. "Water take me far. Make me forget." He tapped his head. "Live with Choctaws. Then I remember. Not long back, I remember all. Come look for you."

"Lost your pony too?"

"Find yours dead." Before I could ask, he added, "No saddle, no gold."

The door opened, spilling a rectangle of yellow light across the hardpan. Despite her fear of Indians, Ruth came out carrying two cups and the coffeepot. She kept her eyes averted from Charlie as she set the pot down. "If he's hungry, we have plenty," she said to me.

He grunted. "Food sound good."

She looked around at him.

He pointed to his chest. "Me good Injun. Good Injuns hungry too." He chuckled.

Ruth smiled shyly. "I'll bring some. You want some too, Martin?"

Reluctantly, I nodded.

Charlie watched her closely. After she went back inside the cabin, he muttered. "That one shoot at me?"

"No." I chuckled. "Her sister. The woman has a big hate for all Indians. Stay away from her."

"Not worry. Me born in the woods. Owl no scare Charlie."

Charlie was always coming up with sayings, most of which I never understood. I just agreed with him and got on with the business at hand. Quickly, I filled him in on what had taken place with me. He nodded when I told him about Big Tree.

"Then that was you across the river."

"Big Tree lucky." He patted his Sharps rifle. "This put big hole in buffalo. Bigger hole in Big Tree."

The Sharps was a formidable weapon. Sometimes called a Beecher's Bible because Henry Ward Beecher had once sent box loads of Sharps to the abolitionist, John Brown—labeled BIBLES,—the rifle was accurate up to a thousand yards. Billy Dixon proved that at Adobe Walls. Some claim his shot was over 1500 yards. That was hard for me to believe, but he did hit that Comanche out there.

I laughed. "It's good to have you here. We'll stay in the barn tonight." I hooked a thumb toward the house. "There's a bunch of women inside. Like I said, one hates Indians. Two are not right in the head. They good women, but the Great Spirit has taken part of them. This last one understands, I think."

He nodded briefly, giving no sign of any concern.

"Why didn't you come over last night?"

"I follow Big Tree. They head southwest. I think they make big circle and come back. They go on, all but three who come back." He spread the fingers on his hands several times. "They come back. Take many cattle last night. Cross river into Choctaw country." He indicated northeast.

By now the sun had peeked above the horizon. I drained my coffee and pushed to my feet. "Wait a minute."

Back inside, Deborah glared at me. I didn't know if it was because I had been talking to an Indian or she still remembered our confrontation behind the barn. I couldn't understand that kind of hate because nothing good could come from it.

I tried to put them at ease. "You don't need to worry about Charlie. He's been with me for years. He was going back to East Texas with me and help me get my uncle's plantation back on a paying basis." I nodded to the shotgun in Deborah's hands. "You can put that down. Now, how many head of cattle do you run here?"

She frowned. The furrows across her forehead looked like a freshly plowed field. "Why do you want to know that?"

I grinned at the suspicion in her tone. "Charlie was hiding across the river yesterday when Big Tree was here. He followed them, figuring they might double back. They kept going, but three left during the night and according to Charlie, rustled some of your cattle. They're pushing them northeast, into Indian Territory. They've already crossed the river."

"What?" A flush of rage colored Deborah's face. "Is he sure?"

"He's sure they took some cattle. He doesn't know if they're yours or not, but seeing as there's not another ranch within twenty miles either way, I got a feeling they belong to you ladies."

She slapped a battered hat on her head. "Well then, let's go find out."

I had the chestnut pony Ruth had loaned me. Deborah was forced to give Charlie a pony. I figured it must have really chapped her good, but she didn't have a choice. He was the only one who knew where the rustling took place.

Two hours later, we arrived at the spot.

"They ride there," Charlie said, pointing northeast.

We studied the sign. "How many head of cattle?"

Deborah studied the cattle grazing in the distance. "Hard to say, but from the way the ground's tore up, I guess sixty, seventy head. I had about a hundred head out here."

Charlie nodded and once again held up the fingers on both hands several times.

I spotted a cloud of dust back south. "Reckon that's your trail herd. Good thing we got here when we did. Few more hours, all sign would have been wiped out."

"Looks that way," she replied, gazing anxiously after the rustled cattle, then back at the approaching herd.

My arm ached despite the fact it was healing well. I popped a clove of peyote in my mouth and chewed it. "Let's get ourselves back to the ranch. Charlie and me will provision up and run your herd down. If we move fast enough, we can get them before they have a chance to sell'em off or butcher them."

She shot a malevolent look at Buckskin Charlie who simply sat in his saddle staring after the rustled cattle, ignoring her completely. She glared at me. "How do I know you'll come back? You could sell'em and keep the money for yourself."

Nodding agreement, I grinned at her. "Reckon you're right, Miss Deborah. Now I know you have a low opinion of men. Personally, it makes me no difference what caused it, but right now, you're faced with a choice of taking care of this trail herd moving up or going after your cattle. If it'll make you rest easier, take care of the herd then trail after us. Ride down river, and we'll leave sign where we crossed."

"You could leave a false trail."

I shook my head and wheeled my pony about. "I feel sorry for you, Miss Deborah. You think ill of everyone. You must be a mighty lonesome woman."

The angry frown on her face was plug ugly. Her eyes bulged, her nostrils flared out. Finally, she yanked her pony around and dug her star-roweled spurs into the unlucky animal's flanks.

As I watched her race away, I wondered if I might not be smarter if I just rode on out to East Texas.

Thirty minutes after we reached the ranch, Charlie and me headed east along the riverbank.

I glanced over my shoulder. We were traveling light, our provisions stashed in two flour sacks draped over my pony's rump and tied to the cantle of my saddle.

The day was hot and still. The baking sun pulled the moisture from the riverbank in steamy clouds that almost took your breath away. From time to time, we rode into the river to cool off, constantly aware of the treacherous quicksand for which the Red River was well known.

An hour later, Charlie pointed out my dead pony far up on the riverbank. The critters had been busy at work on the unfortunate animal. Bare bones glistened whitely through the gaping holes in the roan skin.

I looked upriver, toward the Winkler ranch and thought about my six thousand in gold coin and my books. Somewhere between here and there, they lay. With a grimace, I shook my head. The gold and books might as well be on the moon.

Another hour passed before we cut the rustlers' trail and crossed the river.

The sun was dropping low, so despite my uneasiness about caves, we found a snug one on the north side. While I built a small fire, Charlie found us a fat rattlesnake. The white meat popped and crackled on spits around the fire. I ate my fill, grateful I wasn't faced with the ubiquitous corn mush or Miss Ruth's stew.

During the night, I awakened to find Charlie's blankets empty. A few hours later, he returned. As he slid into his blankets, he said. "They half-day ahead. We catch tomorrow."

We caught up with them like Charlie predicted, but it did us no good.

Chapter Six

The early morning prairie spread vast and empty before us. The only sound was the squeaking of leather, the muffled grunt of our ponies in a high lope, and the hiss of hooves digging into sand.

Mid-morning, gunfire echoed across the rolling prairie. Charlie and me exchanged puzzled looks. Easing forward to the crest of a sandhill, we squinted into the distance. All we saw was more rolling prairie scarred by stands of stunted trees along shallow watercourses meandering through the broad valley below.

Urging our ponies forward, we crossed the valley cautiously, our eyes constantly moving, scanning the countryside surrounding us. From time to time, a rabbit bolted from beneath our feet. Overhead, hawks soared, chased by pesky sparrows. Everything seemed natural, and that scared me.

Thirty minutes later, we pulled up below the crest of a hill and dismounted, scooting on bellies to the summit. We peered into the valley below. I grimaced.

At the base of the hill, six Indians lay sprawled in the sand and grass, carrion for the several buzzards hopping around among the bodies. Beyond, the ground was torn by the hooves of beeves pushed west by the jaspers who killed the braves. We rose to our feet, frightening away the buzzards.

"Scavengers," I remarked, noting the shod hoof tracks.

Charlie grunted. "Sell to herd."

"Probably." It was an old practice, offering a trail herd stolen beeves. Some trail bosses added a hundred or more head to their herd for the price of ten. And both sides were content.

"More than we thought," I said, nodding to the six dead Indians. "Must have picked up those three. What are they, Caddo?"

"Choctaw."

"You sure? Looks Caddo to me."

Charlie shook his head emphatically. "Choctaw."

I didn't argue. Around this part of the country, a body was likely to see every tribe from Comanche to Cherokee. When the Indian Territory was formed, the government assigned each tribe a parcel. The Territory itself was a small fragment of the original hunting grounds each tribe had once ruled, and forcing so many tribes into such a small area assured a blurring of boundaries. To run across a band made up of Caddo, Cherokee, Choctaw, Kiowa, and Comanche wasn't unusual.

Overhead, the buzzards circled. "Look at 'em," I growled. "Just waiting for us to leave."

We rode out, following the rustlers.

We caught them when the red ball of a sun was hand high above the western horizon. There were eight cowpokes, down-at-the-heel rawhiders. Four to one odds didn't set too well with me, not unless I had an advantage to offset their numbers.

And at that moment, I didn't have the advantage.

From behind boulders on the peak of a rocky hill, we watched. The herd had cut due north, into a lush countryside that gave mute evidence of a major burn the year before. Belly-high grass covered the valley. The blackened skeletons of trees dotted the landscape, broken limbs pointing like black fingers in every direction.

Just before sundown, a handful of warriors rode in from the west pushing several more cattle. There followed a short period of wild gesticulating, a few rifles changing hands, and then the warriors rode out.

Beside me, Charlie grunted.

I studied the herd. There appeared to be half again the number the Kiowa had rustled from the Winklers.

* * *

After the rustlers made camp for the night, Charlie and me eased back a mile or so, building our own fire in a shallow ravine cut by run-off water. We broiled another rattler.

"We can't afford to go in shooting tonight. The cows would stampede all over the Indian Nation. We'd never get them all."

Charlie's teeth gleamed whitely in the reddish-orange firelight as he grinned evilly at me. He palmed his knife. "You, me, we take two sentries tonight. Then I take care of others." He eyed my bad arm.

I knew what he was wondering. "Yeah. I can take care of one of them."

"Good. Snakes do all of rest of job."

I washed down the rattlesnake with a swig of water from the canteen. "Snakes?"

He nodded briefly, his eyes glittering in amusement. Then I understood.

Charlie dumped the provisions from one flour sack into the other. He held up the empty sack. "I go now." He paused and grinned at me. "You go with me?"

I snorted. "Forget it. I'm not going out there," I replied, trying to still the fear churning in my stomach. There was no way I was going out into the night with him to catch rattlesnakes. Those poisonous little beasts hunt at night. That's why I never cared much for traipsing about the prairie after dark.

If I had to be out after dark, I preferred a nice, hot

fire, and even then, on occasion, a snake slithered into camp, which naturally stirred up a heap of fast dancing, excited cursing, and hurried gunshots.

But tonight, I had no choice. When Charlie returned, we had to go back into the night. We were guessing no more than two nighthawks would be guarding the herd. My job was to take one while Charlie did the other.

I was going to be on foot, with the snakes. I closed my eyes, wishing I had a bottle of Old Orchard whiskey. Half of it to calm my nerves, the other half for the snake bite.

Charlie returned an hour later, the flour sack squirming with angry rattlesnakes. We packed up, put out the fire, and rode out. Charlie held the sack of rattlers away from his pony. While a bite wouldn't kill the mustang, it would spook it enough to cause a commotion.

Just below the crest of a hill overlooking the sleeping herd, we dismounted. I cringed when my feet touched ground. My heart thudded in my chest. I tried to work up a mouthful of saliva for my dry throat, but nothing came up.

I spotted my nighthawk, a vague shadowy figure near a burned tree. Silently, I crouched down into the tall grass. I had shot men before—in the war, rustlers, warring Indians. I don't know for a fact if I killed any, but I had never stalked a soul with the intention of killing him as I was now doing. To be honest, I didn't know if I could follow through with my job or not.

And working with one arm didn't help.

After all, we're only talking about cows, I told myself as I slipped through the tall grass. Yet, those very cows could be the salvation of the women back at the ranch. Back in the east, hanging a horse thief was unheard of, but in the west, a man's life depended on his horse. Stealing it was like depriving him of his own life. Cattle rustling was no different.

I forced those thoughts from my head and paid attention to the task ahead of me. The cowpoke was slumped forward in the saddle, less than ten yards distant, facing away from me. He was close enough. I knew I couldn't miss with my knife.

Rising slowly, I drew my arm back, took aim, then hesitated. Now, I told myself. Do it now. I took another deep breath and then hurled the knife. At that moment, the pony started, throwing the nighthawk backward. The butt of the knife hit him in the back of the head, knocking him off the frightened pony.

Cursing, I grabbed the .36 Navy and rushed forward, planning on walloping him across the temple.

The cowpoke staggered to his feet, addled. His pony squealed and bolted. When he saw me charging him, my handgun over my head, the nighthawk turned and ran. He suddenly stumbled and fell forward only to jerk to a halt as he impaled himself on the spear-like point of a blackened limb broken by the fire.

All I could do was stare at him, at the tremors racking his body, at the frantic twitching of his fingers and arms as his dying brain sent out garbled messages. He gurgled, then groaned, then collapsed on the limb.

He was an outlaw, a thief, but deep inside, I couldn't leave him draped on the limb. There was something unclean about such an act. Struggling with my one arm, I pulled him from the limb and laid him on the ground.

The bluish starlight cast shadows over his features, but he didn't look a day over sixteen. I shivered.

Quickly, I made my way back to the ponies where Charlie was waiting for me. I nodded.

Without a word, he picked up the bag of snakes. "You wait. I be back."

On the crest of the hill, I stood beside the ponies, staring down onto the camp. I relaxed. If any snakes were nearby, the horses would sense them first.

Gripping the reins tightly, I followed the vague shadow of Buckskin Charlie ghosting through the tall grass. Just beyond the camp, he rose, twirled the bag over his head a few times, then hurled it toward the fire.

It tumbled over and over in mid-air and struck smack in the middle of the flames. Coals exploded like a geyser, glittering red sparks boiling up into the black sky.

Rattlesnakes by nature possess an ill temperament. But when you singe their rattles with a hot fire, they explode into frenzy, taking on a detestable and repugnant disposition that even old Beelzebub would envy.

Before the geyser of coals could settle to the ground, half-a-dozen furious rattlesnakes came boiling out, hissing and striking at every shadow, every movement. Rattles whined like a hive of wild bees.

The camp exploded into a melee of screams, shouts, and gunfire. Frightened shadows criss-crossed in every direction. Two cowpokes slammed together, knocking themselves to the ground in the midst of the snakes.

I never believed in the old hokum of levitation, but, screaming at the top of their lungs, those two hombres exploded into the air, and I'll swear, their boots were two feet off the ground when they started running.

Horses squealed and tore away from their tether ropes. Beyond the camp, the cattle bawled nervously. A few broke and ran, but most remained close.

We sat tight, waiting for the commotion below to calm. The cattle had milled about some, but then settled back down. Without any sentries, the animals started drifting, grazing as they went.

Come sunup, we rode into the deserted camp.

"Reckon you and your passel of rattlers did the job up proper, Charlie."

He nodded, then leaned from his pony and scooped an object off the ground. It was a twist of tobacco. Without hesitation, he gnawed off a chunk and handed it to me. I followed his example. It had been a spell since I'd had a dose of tobacco.

"All we need now is a bottle of good whiskey," I drawled as I chewed on the cud of tobacco.

"You not drink what you find here, Wallace. It Injun whiskey."

"Well, then," I replied, "we'd better pull these beeves together and light a shuck out of here before our friends calm down and come back."

We rounded the cattle and pushed southwest, hoping to hit the Chisholm Trail right at Red River Crossing. I counted just over a hundred head of beeves. Not too bad considering all that had taken place.

Of course, I told myself cynically, regardless of how many head we pushed back to the ranch, Deborah would probably claim we sold ten or twenty head and pocketed the money. I shook my head. I indeed did feel sorry for the woman.

I rode drag, from time to time darting to one side of the herd or the other to push drifters back in. Ahead, Charlie rode point. We drifted the cattle southwest lazily, letting them think it was all pretty much their own idea. A healthy beef can graze ten–twelve miles a day without losing weight or feeling stress.

Mid-afternoon, Charlie pulled up and motioned a halt. He rode back. "We go west. Kiowa ride here," he said, pointing in the direction we had been heading.

We cut west. By evening, we hit the Chisholm and turned the beeves south.

"Somewhere down there is a trail herd."

He gestured to a box canyon stuck back in some rocky outcroppings in a shallow ridge west of the trail. "Put animals there."

And that's what we did, after which we made a camp in the mouth of the box canyon.

Next day, we hailed the trail herd and sold it forty head of beeves. The other sixty, we pushed back across the Red River with eighty dollars cash.

I wasn't sure what I was expecting when we reached the ranch. But the last thing I would have guessed was that Sarah would have run off with a trail hand from one of the passing herds.

Chapter Seven

Before we had the cattle halfway across the river, Deborah and Ruth emerged from the cabin. They stood in the cool shade of the cottonwoods watching us.

The surprise on Deborah's face was obvious. I grinned to myself, imagining just how much more she would be surprised when I turned the eighty dollars over to her.

But when we pulled up, I was the one who was surprised when I saw the expression on Ruth's face. She had been crying and lines of worry drew her cheeks taut.

She ran up to me and laid her hands on my leg. "Martin. Sarah's gone. She ran off with a drover."

I looked from her to Deborah, who simply shrugged and eyed the cattle. "See you got them all back."

I'd be lying if I said her indifference did not startle me. It did. Her reaction was the last I would have expected, but when I considered the kind of person she was, it fit her perfectly. She was more concerned with cash than family. I pulled the eighty dollars from my pocket and handed it to her. "I'll explain later," I said, motioning Charlie to keep pushing the cattle. I glanced down at Ruth. "I'll be back in a minute. We need to get the cattle out behind the barn. There's graze there."

Ruth stood in front of the cabin, wringing her hands, but Deborah followed us beyond the barn, counting the greenbacks I had handed her.

We turned the cattle loose on some new grass behind the corral and dismounted. I handed my reins to Charlie. "Put the ponies up and throw your soogan in the barn. We'll bunk there."

He grunted. Deborah and I started back to the cabin while I filled her in on all that had taken place.

As we turned the corner of the barn, I saw Ruth staring at us, her arms crossed over her chest and hugging herself.

Deborah patted the pocket into which she had slid the greenbacks and gave a short laugh. "Not a bad day's work," she muttered, stepping around Ruth and disappearing inside without even a thank you or go to blazes.

"Now, tell me what happened," I said to Ruth.

She ducked her head. "We don't know. The herd settled down here for the night before crossing. When we awakened the next morning, there was a note on the fireplace. She was gone. Her gripsack was missing. We saw the trail boss, a man named Ruback. He checked his crew. One was missing, a cowboy he'd picked up in Fort Worth by the name of Will Hamilton." She hesitated, chewing on her lip, trying to hold back the tears. "We just want her back."

I studied her a moment. "Look, if you want, Charlie and me can ride after her. We can find 'em, but. . . ." I paused, not quite sure just how to explain my next thought.

"But what?"

"But, your sister is a woman growed. I don't see how she can be made to come back if she doesn't have a mind to."

Ruth's eyes blazed a moment, then softened. She nodded emphatically. "I know, and you're right, but I guess what we want to know is that she's all right." She shrugged helplessly. "I suppose that's about all we can hope for."

"Yes, ma'am, I suppose so."

She looked over my shoulder and spotted Charlie outside the barn. "Tell your friend he's welcome to share our meal, and he can throw his blankets on the floor in front of the fireplace."

"Why, thank you, Ma'am, but I reckon he'd. . . ."

Before I could finish, she sniffed the air once or twice, and then screamed. "Heavens! The pork. It's burning." She raced back into the house.

"Burned? Pork?" I thought of the bitter stew, of the corn mush, and now we had burned pork. I shook my head and peered into the darkness of the cabin. Miss Ruth was a mighty fine woman, but somebody needed to give her a few hints about cooking.

Deborah opted out of supper, claiming she wanted to look over the stock Charlie and me had brought in. Old Mrs. Winkler sat in the rocker, her knitting in her hands. I didn't think she had any inkling I was back. I studied her a moment, wondering just what she was knitting.

Charlie and I sat on one side of the trestle table and Ruth on the other. She had worked hard on the meal, whipping up a bowl of red-eye gravy to go with the burned pork and corn mush. I know folks sometime joke about meat being like shoe leather, but on my sainted mother's grave, that was the consistency of the pork that night.

I got to hand it to Charlie. He hesitated at the first bite, gave me a puzzled look, and then gamely turned back to his meal when I simply shrugged. He was the perfect supper guest, for he cleaned his plate and even took a chance on seconds, causing Ruth to beam at his appetite.

It was probably the first time in her life anyone had asked for seconds.

Deborah returned just as we were wiping our plates clean. She stood by the fireplace, staring deliberately into the flames. Not a soul in that room, with the exception of poor Mrs. Winkler, knew she wasn't watching the flames. She was waiting for Charlie to leave.

I finished my coffee and rose. Charlie did the same, wiping the back of his hand across his lips and nodding. He headed for the door.

Ruth stopped him. "You can sleep in here tonight, Charlie. In front of the fire."

He halted, then turned slowly, letting his black eyes sweep the room, hesitating only a moment at Deborah, before settling his gaze on Ruth. I indicated the roof. "Obliged, Miss. But, me not feel good in white man's house."

I grinned. I knew the feeling. "Go on, Charlie. I'll be out later."

Ruth glared at Deborah. After Charlie closed the door behind him, she snapped. "I hope you're satisfied, you . . . you. . . ." She sputtered. "Oh, I wish I could cuss."

Deborah's face twisted in anger. "You just better watch your mouth, or I'll. . . ."

"You'll do what?" Ruth jutted her jaw and took a step forward.

And Mrs. Winkler sat between two, rocking and

rocking, knitting on her project slowly, oblivious to the war that threatened to break out around her.

I interrupted. "Calm down, Miss Ruth. It wasn't because of your sister Charlie didn't stay. Me neither. It's just that when you spend all your time outside, a cabin like this seems to press in on a jasper." I patted the sling supporting my arm. "You folks have done right well in doctoring on me. I feel spry as a kitten. I reckon Charlie and me will both sleep better under the stars."

She stared up into my face, her eyes trying read what was in my head. She gave Deborah a wicked glance, then turned back to me. "You sure? Because no one is going tell you where you can't sleep. . . ."

"I'm sure. I'm sure." I glanced at Mrs. Winkler, then Deborah who was still glaring at Ruth. "First thing in the morning, Charlie and me'll ride out and find Sarah for you."

Before I could take a step, Mrs. Winkler spoke up. "Harry, you and your friend can stay in the house if you want to."

Deborah turned her glare to her mother, her lips compressed. She remained silent.

"Thank you, ma'am. But, I like the stars." I glanced at the knitting in her hands, curious as to what she was putting together. It was dark in color, but had no shape that I could see.

* * *

In the barn, Charlie lay on his blanket he had spread in the loft. Moonlight spilled through the open door. I spread my blanket nearby. We lay silently. Finally, he spoke. "Wallace?"

"Yeah?"

"You marry woman?"

"Woman? Marry woman? What are talking about?"

"The small one. You marry her?"

"You mean Miss Ruth? Naw. Where'd you get an idea like that?" He didn't reply, and I continued. "She's mighty fine, but she won't have nothing to do with a worn-out cowpoke like me. Someone like her ought to marry a banker or preacher or someone like that." I fell silent. After a few more moments, I said. "Why are you asking?"

Charlie grunted. "You marry her, you best teach her to cook."

We rode out early next morning, staying west of the Chisholm Trail. I guessed that Sarah and her drover friend would probably head to Fort Sill, which was near the headwaters of Cache Creek.

If we were lucky, we might cut their sign, save us a few days.

We didn't get lucky, so mid-day we cut back west, planning to camp on Little Beaver Creek that night. We stopped early in a small clearing in the middle of a patch of shinnery, wrist-thick oak about eight feet high and growing so close together, a man has to force his body through. We built a small fire, broiled a couple trout Charlie snatched from the creek, and by sundown, had extinguished the fire and rolled up in our soogans while our ponies grazed on the fresh grass we had brought in.

I snapped awake and stared at the stars overhead. It was around four or five, not long until false dawn, but something had awakened me. I whispered. "Charlie?"

A soft grunt told me he was awake.

We both listened.

The night was still, the warm air filled with the musical chirruping of crickets. In the distance, the melancholy howl of a lonesome coyote hung over the tinkling song of the crickets like a nebulous cloud.

I strained to discern sounds beneath the obvious.

There it came again, a soft rustling back in the shinnery, and then a second, from a point opposite the first.

For a fleeting moment, Charlie and I looked at each other, and though our eyes were hidden in the shadows cast by the moonlight, we knew what we had to do.

I shucked my six-gun and eased it onto my chest beneath the blanket. I remained motionless. Slowly, I turned my head to the side so I could watch the shinnery nearest me. The scratching stopped.

An animal? Armadillo maybe? Or possum? They prowled at night, and they made a commotion.

Or Indian?

My heart thudded against my chest, but I forced myself to breathe normally.

After a few moments, the rustling began once again. I peered between almost closed lids. The thickly growing trunks of the shinnery stood out in black silhouette, rows of closely spaced vertical shafts through which I could pick out the moonlit prairie beyond. A straight black line separated the prairie and the shadows cast by the shinnery.

Shinnery grows so thick that no brush, no weeds can grow beneath it. Then I spotted the source of the noise. A black lump the size of a saddle interrupted the line dividing the shinnery from the prairie. If it were an armadillo, it was the biggest I'd ever seen. Too small for a deer, too large for a bobcat.

The dark protuberance moved.

Under the blanket, I cocked the hammer on my .36 Navy.

And waited. I held my breath.

The shadow continued to ease toward me.

The movement was too deliberate, too focused to be anything but a human. Scavengers weren't so patient, nor were Comancheros. So, who in the blazes could—

Without warning, the phantom shadow leaped upright, and I fired. The war cry that came from his lips turned into a cry of pain as the slug knocked him around.

Behind me, Charlie fired, three times, one right after another until they seemed like one report.

Throwing off the blanket for a better aim, I leaped to my feet and cocked the hammer, but the ghostly apparition just as suddenly vanished.

Moments later, a single set of hoofbeats sounded from the night.

Keeping my back to Charlie while I studied the night around us, I whispered. "They gone?"

"Maybe."

"What about yours?"

"Dead."

I relaxed. "Then I think no more around."

We checked. Charlie's was dead, and mine was gone.

"Comanche," he said, staring down at the Indian lying in the moonlight beyond the ring of shinnery.

"Must have spotted us when we camped."

Charlie agreed.

Holstering my handgun, I pulled old man Winkler's hat down on my head and grinned at Charlie. "Since everyone within ten miles knows we're here, I reckon we oughta boil us some coffee and whip up a bite to eat before we pull out."

Chapter Eight

We forded Little Beaver Creek and continued west toward Big Beaver Creek a short distance beyond. Another couple miles beyond, we'd hit Cache Creek, which would lead us into Fort Sill.

I admired the pristine beauty of the stream. My pa always told me I was some kind of dreamer and that sometimes I took a skewed view of that around me. He was right. I never admitted it to him, naturally. Mainly because he was my pa, and like most boys, I wanted to prove him wrong about everything.

He got himself killed in the War of Secession, and in the years afterward, I learned the hard way that he had not been wrong about everything. In fact, there wasn't much that he had not been right about concerning me. There were times I wished I could tell him, but then I reckoned he knew.

So despite the feelings I had against the Indian, Comanche and Apache especially, I couldn't help feeling a mite sorrowful for the way of life they'd lost.

Taking in the beauty of Cache Creek, I could imagine young boys and girls living the wild life, free to do what they could, enjoying the beauty of nature. If they were hungry, they took game. If they were thirsty, they had the sweet cold water of the creeks and rivers.

I paused at a broad pool of clear water, surrounded by cottonwoods on one side and a rocky ledge on the other. In my mind's eye, I saw young Indian boys laughing and shouting as they leaped from the rocky bluff into the icy water.

If a band wanted to move to another location, they moved. Of course, the white people could do the same, but it seemed the Indian had enjoyed a life unfettered by so many of the constraints with which our culture shackled us.

Too bad life had to change, yet I had to admit, much of the change had been for the better. Reckon it generally is, but sometimes a jasper wonders.

We spotted Fort Sill around noon. Down in Texas, I took for granted that the noonday sun was always ten degrees hotter than Hades, but up in the Indian Territory it was even hotter. Heat rose in waves, contorting the fort the way water warps your reflection when you drop a pebble in a pond.

We rode on in.

On two sides of the parade field, stone buildings stood shoulder to shoulder like soldiers at attention. Behind the buildings were the barracks. On the third side of the parade field was the stable, the blacksmith, and the civilian livery. A false-fronted saloon, a clapboard general store, and a stick shack with a sign on it saying Tonsorial Parlor made up the fourth side. By itself on one corner was a tent on which a sign hung stating Western Freight.

Charlie stayed with the ponies while I nosed around. There were always Indians around Fort Sill, so no one took any particular notice as long as they stayed where they belonged, outside.

No one had seen a cowpoke and woman ride in, nor was anyone familiar with the name Will Hamilton.

Before we rode out of Fort Sill, I bought boots, a couple bags of Bull Durham, a slab of bacon, flour, and some canned fruit for the Winklers. As an afterthought, I picked up a bucket of beer for six bits. Even if we'd had no luck finding Sarah, Charlie and me were going to relax around the campfire that evening.

For the next three days, we scoured the countryside for the couple. Not even the two small bands of Indians we ran across had seen any sign of them.

Finally, we cut south for Red River Crossing.

Charlie and me had a good relationship. I did most

of the talking, and he did most of the listening. But, I was smart enough to know that when he spoke, I best pay attention.

Our ponies ambled lazily down a rock-strewn side of a steep hill, from the crest of which we had paused to search the countryside around us in a last, desperate effort to spot anything that might lead us to Sarah.

"The only answer I can come up with is that her and her drover was caught and carried off by one of the tribes."

Charlie said nothing. He continued riding as if I hadn't spoken.

So I continued. "Of course, that don't make a whole lot of sense. Why would they do that? It's usually the youngsters that get carried off. The grownups, they kill. They don't bury them either."

I paused again, and again, Charlie said nothing.

"We covered enough country the last couple days that we'd have spotted something, buzzards, coyotes, something pointing us to them if they was dead."

For several moments, I considered my last observation.

I had to be right. Upon leaving Fort Sill, we had headed north, then swung east in a semi-circle. At the end of the circle, we moved another half-day south and made another semi-circle. Yep. I was satisfied that we had covered the ground thoroughly. If they'd been laying out there somewhere, we would have found them. Since we didn't, I reckoned they were still alive.

Looking out across the vast prairie before us, I nodded. "Yep. I reckon they are still alive somewhere. What do you think?"

Keeping his eyes on the country ahead of us, he finally spoke. "I think we go back to river."

"Then what?"

"We wait."

"How long?"

His shoulders sagged. He did that at times when he was frustrated with me. "As long as we must."

Ruth met us outside the cabin, the disappointment on her face obvious when she saw Sarah wasn't with us. From the open door in the barn, Deborah watched, her dusty, battered hat pulled down over her eyes and a bridle dangling from her hand. Charlie pulled up behind me as I gave Ruth the bad news.

"Nowhere. No one has seen or heard about her."

Squeezing her eyes shut, she ran her fingers through her short hair and hugged herself. "I was afraid of that," she said, looking up at me and blinking the tears from her eyes.

"It don't surprise me." Deborah's rough voice carried across the hardpan as she approached, slapping the end of the reins viciously against the palm of her calloused hand. "I didn't figure you and your Injun friend would find her."

Mrs. Winkler appeared in the doorway to the cabin.

Her vacant eyes suddenly lit when she spotted me. A broad smile spread over her lips, animating her wrinkled face. "Harry. I was so worried about you. You been gone so long." She looked over her shoulder into the cabin. "Sarah. Your brother, Harry, is here. Hurry." She glanced up at me apologetically and held up her hand as if to stay me. "I'll get her, Harry. Don't go away. I'll get her." And she disappeared back into the cabin.

Ruth looked up at me in despair. "She's getting worse each day."

Deborah stopped at her sister's side. "What do you expect? Everything she ever wanted is gone."

"She still has us."

The older sister snorted. "Us? She don't want us. All she ever wanted was Sarah and the boys. She never cared about you and me."

Ruth's eyes blazed. She took a step toward her older sister. "That isn't true. You know better than that."

I felt like the proverbial fly on the wall. But I wasn't about to butt in. If I did, one of them would probably swat me good.

For several seconds, the two sisters stood glaring at each other. Finally, Deborah shook her head. "You wouldn't believe the truth if it jumped out and slapped you in the face." She whipped the reins against her hand to punctuate her declaration. She cut her eyes toward me defiantly, then stormed back to the barn.

Releasing a deep breath, Ruth looked back up at me

and grinned sheepishly. "Sorry about the family squabble."

I dismounted. "Don't be. I wish I had a family to squabble with. By the way," I added, indicating the plunder bag riding on my pony's rump, "I brought some flour and bacon and canned peaches."

Squealing with delight, Ruth clutched the bag to her chest. "I've been dying for peaches. Why, I'm going to make you two a peach cobbler that you'll never forget. Pa and the boys liked it even better than my stew."

Suddenly, I had some serious reservations about having bought her the peaches.

The last trail herd had given the Winklers a hind-quarter of beef, knowing that most ranchers were reluctant to slaughter their own beef for food, yet more than willing to give one to a neighbor if he needed it.

For a few months, I had ridden for an old gent who was one of the first to settle in West Texas. A day's ride south was another ranch, settled at the same time. The two old codgers swapped beef. Neither would kill one of his own, so he killed one of his neighbor's. In turn, when the neighbor ran low on beef, he slaughtered one of the other's. The practice was a way of life. Never made much sense, but then, life in the thirties and forties was a heap more fraught with trouble than it was three or four decades later.

* * *

That night, Ruth made up some boiled beef with succotash, followed with a heaping serving of peach cobbler.

I wouldn't exactly say that Charlie and me approached the supper table that evening with the demeanor of two jaspers climbing the gallows, but it was with some trepidation that we took our places at the table.

The aroma filling the cabin was mouth-watering, sort of like the dark before the storm, I told myself, instantly feeling a pang of guilt for my lack of faith in her culinary skills.

The coffee was hot and black, thick as mud and strong as a trail driver's socks at the end of the trail. The boiled beef was like rubber and the succotash was almost brittle. I was puzzled how one could be cooked too much and another not enough, but with enough salt and honey, we made it through the meal.

The cobbler was watery, the dough doughy, but I could still taste the peaches.

"Delicious cobbler," I said, grinning at Ruth.

She beamed and looked around the table. Deborah choked down another large bite of boiled beef and smacked her lips, but Mrs. Winkler pressed her lips together stubbornly and pushed her plate back and shook her head. "I don't like boiled beef, I told you that."

Ruth glanced at me briefly, an embarrassed blush on her cheeks. She leaned over and patted her mother's hand. In a calm voice, she said. "Yes, you do, Ma. It's pork you don't like. Boiled beef is your favorite. Remember?" She reached for the jar of honey. "Here, let's make it sweeter."

For a moment, I thought her Ma was going to bow her neck, but when Ruth offered her a spoonful of honey, Mrs. Winkler opened her mouth. She rolled her eyes and licked her lips. "Put a lot of honey on the meat."

"Sure, Ma. A lot."

Later, while Charlie and me lay on our blankets outside the barn staring at the stars overhead, I remarked. "I think Miss Ruth and her cooking is getting better."

With a short grunt, Charlie replied. "Than what?"

"You know what I mean. I didn't have to heap as much salt and honey on it this time as before."

We lay quietly for several seconds.

I spoke up again. "Her cooking don't seem to bother her Ma or sister."

"Maybe that why her sister mean as badger and her mother talks to rocks."

Chapter Nine

Hoofbeats awakened me during the night. I sat up, at the same time reaching for my handgun. The moon was behind the cottonwoods, casting shadows across the barn and over Charlie and me. Beyond the shadows, the moon lit the prairie with a bluish glow broken by the stark, black outlines of sagebrush. The broad river looked like a solid band of black, and the hissing rush of water drifted across the empty prairie.

I strained to hear, but the only sound was the river. I placed my hand on the hardpan. There they were, faint vibrations.

Charlie's guttural voice broke the silence. "They ride on. Not come here."

"Who were they?"

"Not know. Comanche, maybe. They fight the bluecoats there," he said, pointing west to the Texas Panhandle.

"That's a hundred, hundred and fifty miles from here."

He lay back and clasped his fingers beneath his head. "Two days for Comanche."

Moments later, he was sleeping.

I lay awake, wondering about the fighting, hoping it stayed where it was. I had seen the war coming during the fight at Adobe Walls. I saw it when Billy Dixon made that spectacular half-mile shot that knocked the Comanche from his pony. I saw it when the local restaurant owner, William Olds, shot himself in the head while clambering down from his lookout at the trading post.

I hoped the Panhandle would contain the war, and leave us be.

The next day, I was seated at the table in the cabin while Ruth checked the dressing on my arm where the broken bone had torn through the flesh. Both the wound and the bone were healing well. She dabbed more of that cottonwood honey on my arm.

The rattle and clatter of a wagon bouncing over the hardpan caused us to look out the window.

A chuck wagon pulled up in front of the cabin. A bandy-legged greasebelly jumped down from the seat and introduced himself. "Name's Elmer Higgs from South Texas. Got three thousand head of ornery beeves a few miles back. Plan on nighting down at the cottonwoods by the river's edge and crossing first thing in the morning. Jess Lambertane's trail boss. Said I could pick up supplies here." He hooked his thumb over his shoulder to the young boy still perched up on the seat. "Got plenty help in loading, so I won't be putting you folks out none."

Deborah led them to the barn and within half an hour, Elmer had his supplies and paid his bill. Touching his fingers to the brim of his once-white Stetson, the greasebelly geehawed his team of four mules a few hundred yards to the river crossing.

Back in the cabin, Deborah announced supplies were running low.

Ruth glanced at her mother, who was rocking in front of the fire. "What are we going to do? Sarah's gone. I can't go off with you and leave Ma here by herself."

Keeping her eyes on her knitting, Mrs. Winkler spoke up in her trembling voice. "Harry can go."

I cleared my throat. "I'd be more than happy to lend a hand."

Deborah eyed me skeptically. She still hadn't forgiven me for our argument out in the corral.

"I'm in good shape, plenty good to drive the wagon into Fort Sill for your supplies. You give me a list, and I'll bring them right back."

Ruth's face lit up. "Why, Martin. That's very. . . ."

"Why would you want to do that?" Deborah interrupted.

"Look, Miss Deborah. I'm not the drifter you think I am. When the flood got me, it took all my money, six thousand dollars, in gold double eagles."

Her eyes grew wide. "Where'd you get money like that?"

"I killed me a heap of buffalo. Sold the hides. Worked hard, then decided to leave. Indian trouble with the Comanche."

I glanced at Ruth whose eyes were riveted on me. "I promised my Pa and my uncle to take care of my uncle's plantation on the Sabine River in East Texas. Yankee carpetbaggers have it now, and they're selling if off fast as they can. I planned to buy back what I could of it." I shrugged. "But the money's gone. And so is the dream I'd held onto for so long."

Skepticism replaced the scowl on Deborah's face.

Clearing my throat, I continued. "I owe you folks. I got no money, but I can work. I want to repay you for what you done for me."

Bouncing from her rocker, Mrs. Winkler turned on us. "Shame on you, Harry. You don't owe us a thing. This is your home." She glared at Ruth and Deborah. "Now, you children stop fighting and help Harry make ready to pick up our supplies."

Her cheeks burning, Ruth turned to Deborah. "Make up the list. Martin and Charlie will get our supplies."

Deborah hesitated. She glanced sidelong at her Ma. "I don't know."

I spoke up. "Charlie can stay here. Look after Miss Ruth and Mrs. Winkler. You and me can go together if that would make you more comfortable, Miss Deborah."

I could see the indecision tumbling about in her head. It had always been my experience that what an hombre figured someone would do to them is usually what he would do to someone else. And I was watching another display of that indecision.

Finally, she made up her mind. "You and Charlie go. I'll make a list and give you the money."

Before she could continue, I said. "And I'll bring you back an itemized list of your goods and what they cost."

She stared at me a moment, unsure as to how to respond. She just nodded.

Later that evening after a supper of cornbread and succotash washed down by hot coffee, Charlie headed back to the barn while I leaned against the hitching rail outside the cabin smoking some Bull Durham tobacco. I kicked myself for not picking up a bottle of Old Orchard whiskey in Fort Sill.

Ruth came out sometime later, drying her hands on her apron. I pushed away from the hitching rail. "Evening, ma'am."

She looked up at me. "It's beautiful out here tonight, isn't it, Martin?"

I studied the stars over our heads. The Milky Way looked like a broad road paved with diamonds stretching from one horizon to the other. "Sure is."

"How's your ma?"

"Sleeping in her rocker."

Neither of us spoke for a few moments until she said. "I appreciate you going to Fort Sill for the supplies. Sure helps us out."

"Happy to, ma'am." A silence fell between us again. In the distance a few cows bawled. "How long you folks been here?"

The pale yellow light from the open window lit her face. She shrugged. "I can't remember when we didn't live here." And briefly, she told me how her ma and pa had settled here before the war and set about building a ranch.

"Pa was helping some Confederates push horses across the river during the war when a Union patrol ambushed them. Pa got killed. Later, Stephen was killed by Comanche. Then Harry—he was ambushed by Indians on the way to Fort Sill. I tried to talk him out of going, but he wouldn't listen. His horse came back with blood on the saddle. That's how we knew something was wrong. Deborah brought him back. That was five years ago. That's when Ma snapped. She hasn't been the same since."

She stared unseeing into the night. I sensed a trace of resignation in her tone. "Tough on you kids."

"Huh?" A small smile leaped to her lips, quickly covering the somber reflection that had been on her face. "Oh, no. Not really. I don't mind. Ma needs help. That's why I'm here. It was my fault Harry got killed."

Several times over the last weeks, I had wondered about the attention she did pay her mother, how she catered to her, refused to argue with her, always tried to pacify her. I knew the old woman was fuzzy in her thinking, but somehow, I had the feeling that wasn't the main reason Ruth looked after her so carefully. But now, I knew. "He was a man growed. I don't see how it could be your fault."

She looked up at me, her forehead wrinkled. "He was the baby of the family, Mister Wallace. I should have insisted he stay here."

She glanced at the small campfire near the barn. Charlie sat cross-legged facing it. The firelight cast dancing shadows across his face. She changed the subject. "I still don't understand why you both don't sleep in the cabin."

I chuckled. "Old habits, Miss Ruth. Old habits."

Tentatively, she said. "Will you look for Sarah again? I mean, in Fort Sill?"

"Yes, Ma'am. I most certainly will." I smiled at her gently. "Don't you worry." I ground my cigarette under the heel of my boot and nodded. "Good night."

She said nothing, just nodded back.

In the barn, I eased my arm from the sling. There was still some pain, but I reckoned enough healing had taken place that it was time for me to start exercising the arm a little.

At breakfast next morning, Deborah announced she was going to Fort Sill with me and Charlie could stay on the ranch.

I could say her announcement surprised me, but it didn't. She trusted no one. "Fine with me. You best ask Charlie. I can't speak for him." I knew he would be agreeable, but she needed to ask instead of ordering folks around.

Charlie nodded. "I stay."

Deborah and me rode out later that morning, her handling the wagon, me on my chestnut pony. I kept my arm in the sling for the most part, removing it occasionally to work at the stiffness in it.

We made good time, fording the Red and cutting west along the north bank until we hit Cache Creek, which we followed to the fort. Along the way, we spotted two or three small bands of mounted Indians, but they remained too distant to discern if they wore war paint or not.

I don't reckon there was more than half-a-dozen words said between us for the next two days, but we worked well together. She did her share of camp chores and never once acted as if I should treat her any way except as a working partner.

Truth of the matter is, I'd much prefer Miss Deborah over some riding partners I've had.

Fort Sill was bustling. It must have been just after payday for the troops filled the saloons and lined the boardwalks. We loaded up the wagon, lashed the supplies down, and covered the whole load with a heavy duck tarp. I couldn't find any Cooper books, or *Robinson Crusoe*, so I picked up a couple dime novels just to have something to read.

Then we started questioning every soul at the fort. We began at the livery. Miss Deborah went one direction around the square, and I went the other.

I was in the Bullbat Saloon listening to the tinny pounding of the piano and enjoying a mug of cool beer when Miss Deborah burst through the swinging doors. "Wallace. I found her. She's just north of town."

Chapter Ten

Dust billowed from under our feet as we hurried across the parade field to the wagon. "The old man who owns the dry goods store saw her last week. She bought some . . . some ladies' garments. She told him she was staying with a family by the name of Ledoux north of here, near a fork in the road."

"That's good news," I replied, swinging into the saddle, at the same time noticing the sense of excitement she seemed to be doing her best to suppress.

"Yeah." She looked at me and almost grinned.

Thirty minutes later, we spotted a ramshackle clapboard house west of the fork in the road. The house sagged against an old elm. A bare-bottomed child played in the dirt in front of the open door. As we pulled up, a worn-out woman with her prematurely graying hair pulled back in a severe bun appeared in the door, wiping her hands on a dirty dishtowel with frayed ends. Judging from the age of the tiny child in the dirt, the woman was twenty-four or-five going on fifty.

The West did that to many women.

She eyed us suspiciously.

"Mrs. Ledoux?"

Her eyes narrowed. "Who wants to know?"

I introduced us. "We're looking for a young woman by the name of Sarah Winkler."

"My sister," Deborah put in, the expression on her face hard.

I kept a pleasant grin on my face. "Back in town, they said she was living out here. We were buying supplies and figured on paying her a visit. It's been a spell since she left home."

She studied us a moment. "How do I know you are who you say?"

From the corner of my eye, I saw Deborah half-rise from the wagon seat, then drop back. Hastily, I replied. "Like I said, this is her sister. She has another and her old mother back on the Red River. Who else would we be?"

For several moments, she looked us over. "Reckon it won't do no harm to tell you." She paused, glanced over her shoulder into the dark room behind her, then said. "She ain't here. Left a week or so back. She and that worthless man of hers was going back east to Fort Arbuckle to look for a bullwhacking job."

I glanced at Deborah, but the expression on her face remained as stony as before. Without a word, she climbed down from the wagon and laid her hand on my reins. "I'm going after her. You take the wagon back to the ranch."

"Look, Miss Deborah. You can't. . . ."

Her eyes blazed. "Wallace, you got a bad arm. I worked too hard setting it to want to bust it again, but if you don't climb off that cowpony, that's exactly what I'll do. I'm bigger than you, and I ain't all stove up."

For a moment, I considered arguing with her, but when I eyed the hogleg on her hip and the Winchester in the boot, I figured whomever she ran into out there was the one who needed to worry. And she was right as rain. Right now, she could probably tie a knot in my tail.

The smartest move for me was to get the supplies back to the ranch. Then I could come back.

An hour later, I was plumb tickled I decided not to argue with her. My arm was throbbing until I thought the whole thing would fall off. Handling the ribbons on a four-up demands coordination between the fingers of each hand, and those on my left felt like thick lumps of coal. Hot pain surged through them, coming to an abrupt halt in the fingertips.

Outside of Fort Sill, I pulled off beside Cache Creek and bathed my arm in the cool water. Slowly, the throbbing subsided. I camped early that night, eager to rest the arm. I figured two more nights before I reached the river.

The second night is when the highbinders hit.

Throughout the second day, I pulled up several times to bathe my arm in the creek. At the noon break, the hair on the back of my neck bristled. I looked up and spotted a shadowy figure vanish behind a boulder on the rocky hill some distance from me.

Rising to my feet, I stretched and yawned, making a show of giving the countryside a lazy examination. The truth is, I was peering into every niche, every shadow for whatever I had earlier spotted.

Nothing. At least not at that moment.

From time to time the remainder of the day, I caught glimpses on dark figures among the boulders. Indians? I had no way of knowing.

I made early camp, picking my spot, a clearing surrounded by a meandering creek on one side, and thick growths of wild azaleas and willows—wrapped in berry briars—on the other. I parked the wagon beside one patch of azaleas and tossed my bedroll beneath the wagon.

Knowing I was being watched, I tried to be as nonchalant as possible while I quickly tended the animals and boiled a pot of coffee over a small fire. I figured whoever was stalking me would make no move before dark, but that didn't prevent goosebumps from popping up on my arm.

I opened a can of peaches and speared them with my knife. At dusk, I crawled under the wagon and into my bedroll. Soon crickets began chirruping. As the fire burned down and shadows crept across the camp like skulking cats, I rolled from my blankets into the azalea. I winced as I rolled over a thorn. My hip burned for a moment, but I ignored it.

From there, I slithered on my belly into a pocket of small boulders a few feet beyond the undergrowth.

To my ears, I sounded like a wounded buffalo, but the crickets continued their song, so I knew whoever was out there had heard nothing.

They did not make their move until well past midnight.

The fire was now only a bed of red coals winking in the darkness. Crouched behind a boulder, I heard a rustling beyond the clearing. Rising, I leaned against the boulder, careful not to disturb any of the smaller shards of granite lying on top. I squinted into the night. A vague shadow faded into the underbrush.

I dragged my tongue over my dry lips and flexed my fingers around the butt of the .36 Navy. Off to my left, a branch snapped. I stiffened.

Then a soft voice froze me in my tracks. "Don't

move a muscle, cowboy." The cold muzzle of a revolver pressed against the back of my neck.

I croaked. "I don't plan to." But, my brain was racing. They were smarter than I expected. Seems like I was developing a habit of underestimating my opponents.

I wasn't green enough to believe they'd leave me unharmed. Highbinders wanted no witnesses. Why this jasper hadn't already put a slug in my head, I couldn't figure out, but I was grateful.

"Hand me that hogleg over your shoulder, and slow."

With my back to him, I quickly shifted the Navy Colt to my left hand and grabbed a hand-sized slab of granite that had split from the boulder.

"Here you are," I mumbled, extending the handgun over my left shoulder. "Take it." Then I dropped it down my back and spun, swinging the slab of granite around like a singletree.

The falling six-gun distracted him just long enough. I slammed the granite into the side of his head, and he dropped like a pole-axed hog.

For a moment, I remained motionless, listening for any indication his partners had heard the commotion. Nothing. Only the crickets.

I slung his gunbelt over my shoulder and hefted his .45 a couple times before dropping it in my holster. I felt more secure then, a .36 Navy in one hand and a Colt .45 on my hip. Silently, I eased toward the creek.

Without warning, a single gunshot broke the stillness of the night and something tugged at my shirtsleeve. A plume of orange pinpointed the gunman. I snapped off two shots, then dropped into a crouch and skittered sideways.

A shout of pain sounded from the dark, and the splashing of feet through the creek told the highbinder wasn't waiting around.

I dropped to one knee and waited. Moments later, a single set of hoofbeats echoed through the night followed a couple minutes later with another set.

The silence of the night slowly returned to normal. In the distance, night birds called. And closer in, crickets took up their song once again.

Silently, I wove my way through the underbrush and boulders back to where I had left the first hombre. He had vanished.

With a wry grin, I made my way across the creek and found a small hideaway that gave me a good view of the camp. I didn't sleep the remainder of the night.

Come false dawn, I knew that no one was around, but I still cast a wide swing around the camp, making dead sure that I was right. I found a few blood spatters in the sand where that one jasper had tied his pony. One of my slugs must have struck home.

After a quick breakfast, I moved out, favoring my arm.

*   *   *

That last night was uneventful, and I reached the Red at midday.

To my surprise, the last few miles before reaching the Red River, I got some butterflies in my stomach in anticipation of seeing Ruth again. It was a strange feeling, one I'd never before experienced.

I was puzzled. I'd been around women some. I wasn't what you would call a lady's man by any stretch of the imagination, but I'd rubbed shoulders with hurdy-gurdy dancers as well as temperance ladies. I'd had dealings with many different types of the female persuasion, so I didn't figure I was completely ignorant of them, but none of them had ever made me nervous like I was then.

And what was so odd about the whole matter was that I had the distinct feeling that she just tolerated me, nothing more.

Chapter Eleven

I remember the feeling after the War of Secession when I pulled up at the end of the lane leading to our small farm and saw our cabin still standing.

The tension and fear with which I had lived for four years seemed to just flow out of my veins, replaced with a sense of warmth and security.

It was mighty fine to be home even if I was there all by myself. Pa was dead, Ma had died years before; I was all that was left. Still, it was home.

Or so I thought until I spotted the thin tendril of white smoke drifting into the still air from the chimney.

Frowning, I rode forward.

A tall, angular, shifty-eyed cowpoke stepped from

the door, an 1860 Spencer seven-shot carbine in his hands. He nodded. "How do."

I nodded back, uncertain just as to my next step. "Howdy."

"Travelin' through?

"Not exactly." I gestured to the cabin. "I live here. Or I did. My pa's place before the war."

He studied me carefully. "Your name Wallace?"

"It is."

"Well, Mister Wallace, I bought the place two year back. Taxes was owed. Sheriff put it up for sale. You can check county records."

I knew a passel of homesteads had been sold. We'd heard of the practice while we was fighting up in Missouri and Kentucky. I never figured ours would be one of them. "They was in an almighty hurry to sell it. We paid the taxes in '60."

He tilted the muzzle of the Spencer upward slightly. "I don't want no trouble. I done bought this here parcel fair and square. I'll fight to keep it."

I didn't like the idea of losing the place. I stared back at him, ready to fight myself.

At that moment, a tow-headed youngster around seven stuck his head out the door. "Pa, Ma says to invite the stranger to supper."

That cooled me off right fast. I declined the invitation.

I stopped by Injun Bayou just to be sure the old boy was telling me the truth. He was. The place had been sold for taxes. On top of that, I learned that parcels of my uncle's plantation were also being sold.

I headed west, looking for a bucket of gold.

But now, as I gee-hawed the mules from the river, the Winkler cabin looked just as inviting to me as my pa's once had.

Buckskin Charlie, Ruth, and Ma Winkler were waiting outside the cabin. Ruth's smile faded when she failed to spot Deborah. "She's all right," I said, reining the mules up.

Her smile returned.

"She took up Sarah's trail in Fort Sill. I figured to get your supplies back, then head back to give her a hand if need be."

Mrs. Winkler's wrinkled face beamed. Tears glittered in her eyes. In her hand, she carried a partially knit sweater. "You all right, Harry? You didn't get hurt or nothing, did you?"

"No, ma'am. I'm just fine." I popped the reins against the mules' rumps. "Charlie and me'll unload your supplies."

Ruth clapped her hands. "Good. And to celebrate your return, I'll fry us up some steak and red-eye gravy along with some hot biscuits."

I forced a grin. "Sounds tasty, ma'am. Mighty tasty."

Charlie rolled his eyes.

To my surprise, the fried steak and red-eye gravy

wasn't too bad. Not good, but not like before. Being the gentlemen we were, Charlie and me downed the meal gamely.

Next morning before sunrise, I saddled up a line-back dun and rode out for Fort Sill, hoping to pick up Deborah's trail. I didn't reckon she would be hard to follow, for a woman in farmer's overalls sitting astride a pony would be a sight no jasper would likely forget.

I was right. I cut east at Ledoux's place north of Fort Sill. Ten miles out, I came upon a stick shack covered with hides near a small stream. Deborah had passed that way four or five days earlier.

The next day at Mud Creek, I picked up information that sent me northeast to Wild Horse Creek. Two days later, I ended up at Fort Arbuckle. To my disgust, I learned she had pulled out the day before.

"Reckon she be heading to the Washita River," the blacksmith drawled.

I leaned up against the hitching rail and rolled a cigarette while he checked my pony's shoes. "What's at the Washita?"

He glanced at me and replied in a tone that said I should have known. "Why, follering her sister and the hombre with her. He come here looking for a bull-whacking job. Weren't none around, so they headed for the Washita River."

The new information gave me cause to wonder. Now what was Sarah and her man up to? Did they plan to go down the Washita to Preston on the Red River? From there, Fort Worth was only a short ride.

Next day, I hit the Washita and turned south.

Except for a lucky break, I would have ended up in Fort Worth, two or three hundred miles south of Deborah.

Fort Washita, situated three days southeast of Fort Arbuckle, maintained a landing on the eastern bank of the river. As I rode past on the west bank, I spotted a barge unloading supplies.

Both my pony and me were ready for a rest, so I decided to noon there. While sipping coffee and gnawing on beef jerky, I idly watched the soldiers hefting boxes into the wagons and tying them down.

Then the thought hit me. What if Sarah and her man had swung by Fort Washita? What if they never planned to go to Preston and Fort Worth?

I had my answer after a short swim across the river.

"Yes, Sir." A weathered sergeant growled as a wizened little corporal looked on curiously. "I seen that woman ride into the fort this morning just as we pulled out. Don't reckon I'd care to tangle with her. I. . . ."

"She was mighty mean-looking, she was." The corporal interjected.

The sergeant gave his subordinate a look of irritation. "Yeah. Yeah, I was going to say that, Corporal."

A surge of excitement rushed through my veins. "What about a black-haired woman and a cowpoke? See anyone like that?"

The sergeant replied. "No. Don't reckon nobody come in. I. . . ."

The corporal butted in. "Yeah, you did, Sarge. A woman come in. Remember? Two days ago. Remember? Black hair. She hoofed it into the fort just before dark. She. . . ."

The sergeant cut his eyes at the corporal, aggravated by his inferior's constant interruptions. "Yeah. Now I remember. Rode out next morning. She. . . ."

The corporal beamed. "And she seemed looney."

"Yeah, looney," the sergeant said.

By now, like a horse with the bit in his teeth, the corporal had control of the conversation. "And she headed northeast."

"Yeah. Northeast," replied the sergeant, the scowl on his face deepening.

Oblivious to the sidelong glances of the sergeant, the corporal continued. "Can't figure why, though."

"Nothing out there," added the sergeant. He smiled smugly, finally having the last word.

"Yep. Nothing at all," said the corporal.

I clicked my tongue and rode for the fort.

Deborah's trail was plain as footsteps in the snow. Leaving Fort Washita, she headed northeast toward Sans Bois Mountain. I'd never ridden that part of the Indian nations, but I was told I'd be facing a couple days of dry trail between Boggy River and Sans Bois.

A few miles out of the fort, I ran across an old

camp. From the sign, I realized this was where Sarah met up with her man. The fresher sign around the camp could only belong to Deborah.

By now, I figured I was probably within shouting distance of her, but darkness rolled in, and I bedded down for the night.

An hour after sunrise, I heard gunfire.

Chapter Twelve

I reined up and stared out over the prairie, trying to determine the location of the firing. With a click of my tongue, I headed for the rise before me, figuring on getting a better look from there.

Dismounting before I reached the crest, I crawled the rest of the way on my hands and knees, dropping to my belly when I saw the valley before me.

Less than a hundred yards distant, Deborah lay behind the chestnut pony, her Winchester propped on the dead animal's belly. She fired deliberately, coolly at a band of eight charging Indians. Three more lay sprawled on the prairie.

From where I watched, I couldn't determine the tribe, but from the paint on the war ponies and the way the warriors wore their hair, I guessed the war party was a mixture of three, maybe even four tribes.

Fifty yards from Deborah, half the warriors pulled up. The other four continued the charge, yelping and firing. Instantly, I saw what they planned to do. Charge past, then force her to fight two sides, one unprotected.

With a wry grin, I shook my head and hurried back to my dun. The charging braves should end up just beneath the crest of the hill behind which I was hiding.

I reckoned they were in for a surprise.

The yelping ceased. They were bunching for a final charge against her, four from one side and four from the other. I clanked a fresh cartridge in the Winchester chamber and took a deep breath.

"Let's get them, boy," I yelled at my pony, at the same time digging my heels into his flanks.

He leaped forward, quickly cresting the hill and dropping down toward the warriors who jerked around in confusion to see where the shout had come from.

I came over the hill firing.

Their horses reared, startled. The braves fought to control the animals, but my slugs blistered their hides, and the frightened animals bolted, running into each other.

Deborah turned her rifle on the other four.

I fired as fast as I could lever shells into the chamber. I caught one warrior in the chest, sending him somersaulting off the back of his war pony.

The other three headed out in three different directions.

Her four must have decided the odds had changed too much for they wheeled about and headed north.

I reined up beside the dead pony. Deborah, her face smudged and grimy, nodded to me. "Never thought I'd say it, but I'm mighty glad to see you, Wallace."

"You hurt?"

She shrugged and gave me a rueful grin. "Only my pride. Nothing else."

I scanned the prairie around us. A hundred or so yards away, an Indian pony grazed, the braided rope used for a rein dragging on the ground. Back northeast a half-mile or so, a second pony nuzzled the bear grass.

"Pull your rig off your pony while I get you another one."

The Indian pony was green broke and didn't take too kindly to a saddle, but Miss Deborah stayed with him, and after a dozen or so sunfishes and crowhops, he settled down.

She pulled up beside me. "Thanks again, Wallace. You saved my bacon."

I grinned. "Don't mention it. By the time we find your sister, you might have the chance to save *my* hide."

The smile faded from her face. "If we find her."

"What do you mean? We will."

She indicated a dead Indian. "That war party came from the northeast, the direction Sarah and that drover was taking."

"They might have missed them."

"Maybe."

We took up the trail. Off to our left about fifty yards, the stray war pony watched us curiously. The war paint on him indicated his owner was Kiowa. He still wore the blanket saddle. Deborah and I spotted the patch of black hair dangling from the saddle at the same time.

"Is that what I think?" She pulled up, her face grim.

We both stared at the black object. A sinking feeling stirred in my stomach. I knew exactly what it was. Hair. A scalp. "I'll see."

She stopped me. "No. I'll go. Maybe the horse won't spook if I go over on this Indian pony."

Moments later, she returned, her eyes filled with tears and her face grim. It was a scalp, fresh. The hair would dangle almost to a woman's waist, like Sarah's.

We looked at each other. "I'm sorry," I whispered.

She set her jaw, then gently rolled the hair into a ball and handed it to me. "Put it in the saddlebags. I'll take it back with us."

She looked on silently as I retied the bags.

"Now," she said, her voice growing cold and hard. "Let's see if we can find her and give her a decent burial."

A few miles farther, we spotted circling buzzards. A gorge rose in my throat. More than once, I'd witnessed buzzards' work. I knew it was an essential part of nature, but that made it no less repulsive.

We reined up on top of the bluff overlooking the dry creek bed several feet below. In the middle of the bed lay the drover. The buzzards had done their usual efficient job on the poor jasper.

Deborah twisted on her pony. "I don't see Sarah."

It was impossible to read sign in the sandy bed. Pony hooves and buzzard claws had obliterated any evidence of Sarah.

We rode down into the creek bed. "Head down the creek. I'll go up."

Then I noticed several buzzards sitting in a dead elm, their gaunt, drooping heads turned toward a pile of tumbleweeds jammed into a bend in the creek bank. Probably a rabbit hiding inside.

I started past the tumbleweeds when I heard a moan.

I jerked around.

The sound came again, from the middle of the tumbleweeds. Then I glimpsed a small patch of blue calico beneath the dried weeds.

Leaping from the saddle, I frantically tore the tumbleweeds apart in a desperate effort to reach the calico. It was a woman.

Sarah!

She moaned again.

"Here," I shouted. "Here." I yanked away the last tumbleweed and froze. I closed my eyes and muttered a curse. She had been scalped and left for dead. A thick, dirty crust of blood covered her head. A strip of hair just above her ears and around the back of her head was all that remained.

I grabbed my canteen and knelt at her side, gently cradling her in my good arm while I splashed water over her dry lips. Blood oozed from a wound in her chest.

Deborah came sliding to a halt. She gasped. "Dear Lord."

"Cover her head," I ordered, tilting the canteen as Sarah began eagerly gulping the water. I glanced at her bloody skull. We had nothing with which to tend the wound. "We've got to get her back to Fort Washita before infection sets in."

Without warning, Sarah grabbed the canteen and jammed it against her lips, pouring water down her chin and onto her chest. I tired to wrestle the canteen from her, but she resisted with unbelievable strength.

Abruptly, she went limp.

Deborah dropped to her knees beside us and laid her neckerchief over Sarah's head. I inspected the wound in her upper chest. It was deep, but it missed the lungs.

Quickly, I ripped off my own neckerchief and packed it under her dress against the wound. Then I gently lifted her. "Take her until I get on my horse. I'll hold her until we get back to the fort."

Without hesitation, Deborah took her unconscious sister, then helped her up to me.

We reached the fort well after dark. The camp surgeon took Sarah into the infirmary and tended her. Deborah remained with her while I took our ponies to the livery. I fed and tended them, found me a couple generous slugs of whiskey at the sutler's store, then for another two bits, laid my blanket on the hay in the livery.

As an afterthought, I returned to the sutler's where I bought a bottle of Old Orchard and a bundle of meat and bread.

Some time later, Deborah came in. "The doctor said she'll be fine."

"Glad to hear that."

"Reckon she's going to need a wig now." Her tone was a mixture of anger and humor.

"Well, I know that'll be a blow to her feminine ego, but she needs to realize that she's one lucky lady that she'll be able to wear a wig. I get scared thinking just how easily I could have ridden on past that pile of tumbleweeds."

Deborah nodded, a somber look on her face. "I thought about that." She hesitated, then glanced around the livery. "You sleeping here?"

"Reckon so."

"How much?"

"A quarter."

She shrugged. "Two bits? That ain't bad." She turned on her heel and headed for the office. Moments later she returned and spread her blanket in the next stall.

"Here." I handed her the meat and bread. "Got a bottle of whiskey if you're a mind."

She hesitated, then took it from me. "This isn't ladylike, but then I haven't been much of a lady for the last few weeks." She turned the bottle up and took a long slug. And then she devoured her supper.

Later, just before I fell asleep, she spoke up. "Thanks, Wallace."

"You're welcome," I mumbled.

We hung around a couple days. Physically, Sarah weathered her injuries, but the fear and cruelty to which she had been exposed had broken the last of the tenuous grip she had previously held on reality.

She had moved into a world of her own.

On the third day, we paused on the porch of the infirmary after looking in on Sarah. Deborah stared off the southwest. "We need to get on back to the ranch, but she can't ride."

"Let's take a raft down to Preston and pick up a buggy. It'll be easy going along the river bank to your place."

*　　*　　*

We were in luck. The barge that brought the supplies to the army post was scheduled to go down river the next day.

Three days later, we docked in Preston, found a buggy with a patched canopy and worn axles. I wasn't any too keen about it, but it was the only one in town for sale. We stocked up on grub, and before dark, we were five miles upriver.

I hitched the lineback dun to the buggy and threw my saddle on the Indian pony. During the first day's ride, I picked up an itch on the side of my rump. I figured mosquito or chigger. . . .

That night around the fire, I sipped my coffee while Sarah sat smiling at the fire, humming some unrecognizable little tune.

Deborah leaned back against the buggy wheel. "She hasn't said a word since we left Preston."

"Before then even," I corrected her.

"Yes. Even before then." She paused. Her weathered face frowned in puzzlement. She lowered her voice even though Sarah would never have heard us even if we shouted. "You think she's . . . well, you know . . . ?" She couldn't bring herself to say the words so she just touched a finger to her forehead. "Like that?"

"I'm not smart about those things, Miss Deborah. But I reckon this is probably only a passing thing. The shock and all. She'll come around once she gets home where it's all nice and comfortable." I didn't believe a word of what I said, but I figured a little lie that made someone feel better wasn't too sinful.

The second and third day, the itch on my rump grew more irritating. The morning of the fourth day, I felt a small lump under my flesh. Probably some kind of infection I'd have to open and clean.

We broke camp early that morning, pulling out before sunrise. We were anxious to reach the ranch. Deborah had handled the buggy the whole trip, and she did a fine job of it. Sarah simply sat beside her, humming constantly, staring off into space with a big grin on her face.

The last few days had passed without incident, and I couldn't shake the feeling that our good luck had run its course. The closer we got to the ranch, however, the more I began to think I was just piling someone else's manure in my barn for nothing.

My Indian pony perked his ears forward, suddenly alert. I rose in the saddle and squinted across the prairie. I saw nothing, I strained to hear, but the squeaking of the leather rigging on the buggy and the jangling of O-rings as well as the clatter of the buggy made too much noise to hear any but very distinct noises.

I stayed Deborah with my hand and pointed in the direction of the ranch. We sat motionless, listening to the silence filling the hot air. Then a distant pop reached us. Then another, and another followed by a fourth, this one heavier.

She frowned up at me.

I turned back to the faint sounds. Two more pops sounded. "Gunfire," I whispered, shifting in the saddle to take some of the pressure off the lump on my hip.

The muscles in her jaw rippled when she spoke. "Indians?"

"Maybe. Maybe scavengers like I ran into back on Cache Creek. Whatever it is, we best skedaddle along and see about it."

She whipped her pony into a gallop along the sandy riverbank. Sarah clutched the seat rails. The wind whipped under the patched canopy, causing it to balloon. Moments later, a patch ripped loose and began flapping wildly behind the racing buggy.

Because of the worn axles, the tall, thin buggy wheels didn't track straight. Instead, they rattled to one side or the other, causing the buggy to move in a serpentine course that grew even more pronounced with increasing speed.

I'd seen more than one buggy flip when the rear end swung too far to one side or the other.

I kicked the Indian pony into a lope, easing him closer to the buggy. I motioned her to back off on her speed.

The firing grew louder. The reports from Charlie's .52 caliber Sharps boomed above the other reports. There were maybe four or five guns facing him.

In the distance, I picked out the silhouette of the barn and the surrounding cottonwoods.

Motioning Deborah to rein up, I pulled my pony to

a halt. I shucked the Winchester from the boot. "I'll swing around to the west. When I'm ready for you to come in, I'll pump off four or five fast shots. When I see you, I'll turn up the heat. You get Sarah in the cabin."

She eyed me impassively. "Don't worry about us."

That woman had a knack for hiding her feelings behind a blank face. I wheeled the pony around. "Remember four or five fast shots."

Chapter Thirteen

My plan was simple. I hoped to surprise the attackers from the rear. Whenever Charlie's big Sharps fired, their heads would be down. I hoped they were paying more attention to him than their backends.

I winced when I took a step. That lump on my hip was sore as sin. I touched it and grimaced. Even the slightest pressure sent waves of pain down my leg.

Clenching my teeth, I made my way up a shallow gully behind the barn from where I spotted a lanky hombre wearing a wide-brimmed sombrero crouched behind the watering trough at the corral about a hundred yards distant. Comanchero! I wasn't surprised. What did surprise me was there seemed to be only three or four instead of the usual twenty.

His attention was on the cabin. Each time the Sharps

boomed, he ducked, then popped up to fire off a couple rounds.

Next time he ducked, I cut loose with the Winchester, three quick shots. I held high because the 170-grain slugs dropped quickly. I didn't figure I'd be lucky enough to hit him, but if I peppered the trough, he might hastily reconsider his plans.

He reconsidered in a hurry. Even before the last slug slammed into the water trough, he was up and running toward the prairie where he had probably left his pony in the gully that opened into the river.

The firing stopped, both sides trying to get a handle on who had entered the fray. A second sombrero appeared on the far side of the cabin. I sprayed the sagebrush around it with five slugs.

The sombrero vanished.

Moments later, in the midst of gunfire, the buggy, canopy flapping, skidded around the corner of the cabin and rattled to a halt at the door.

I sprayed slugs into the sage again, and Charlie's Sharps boomed.

Two more figures followed the first hombre, staying in a crouch so we couldn't get a good shot at them. Cowards always run when the odds are even.

And that was fine with me.

After turning out the animals, I paused inside the barn and inspected the knot on my hip. It had swollen into a large boil the size of a fifty-cent piece. Then I remembered the thorn I had rolled onto back at Cache Creek a few days earlier.

Inside the house over a cup of six-shooter coffee, I announced that I figured on cutting the boil and draining the pus, but to my horror, Ruth and Deborah wouldn't hear of it. "If it's a boil," Ruth said. "It has a hard core."

"And it won't get well until the core is out," Deborah added.

"What do you mean, out?" For some reason, I didn't like the way she said 'out.' An uneasy premonition filled my head.

"Out. Removed. Taken out."

I looked from one to the other suspiciously, then glanced around. "You ever see a boil, Charlie?"

He looked around from where he was standing guard in the open doorway. "Bad. They tell you true."

Suddenly, the coffee lost its taste. "How do you get the core out?" I asked reluctantly, turning back to Ruth and Deborah.

Deborah shrugged. "Easy. You just pop it out."

"Pop it out?" I frowned at Ruth. That sounded too easy. "What do you mean, 'pop it out'?"

She explained just as if it were an everyday routine around the house. "Nothing to it. You cut the skin and put a heated bottle on it. The bottle just pulls it out."

That didn't seem too bad. "That's it? The bottle just pulls it out. That easy?"

"Well, it does hurt some, but nothing like it will if

you don't get out. This time next week, it'll be the size of your fist."

Well, that gave me pause to ponder. Right now, it was as tender and sore as my busted arm had been. And if it got worse, then—I looked at Charlie. "How do you get one out?"

He pulled his knife and made a carving motion.

I grimaced. The situation was going from bad to worse, from popping to carving.

Ruth took the first step. "Stop thinking about it. Just drop your trousers, and we'll take care of it right now."

"Do what?" I gaped at her in surprise. "Drop my . . . with women around?" I shook my head. I had my dignity to consider. "I can do it. I mean, Charlie and I can do it."

Deborah shook her head. "No. We need Charlie to hold you down."

For a moment, I was speechless, struggling with a slight case of panic. "To hold me what? Why should he have to . . . ?"

Ruth explained patiently as if I were a six-year-old. "The mouth of the bottle is hot. When it touches your skin, you'll jerk and when you do, the bottle slips off the boil. He has to hold you so you won't jump."

By now, I was really having a bad feeling about the whole operation. I shook my head. I didn't know what to say, so I simply said. "I'm not taking off my clothes in front of women."

Deborah snorted. "We won't see nothing we didn't see with our brothers. If you're so worried, keep the long johns on. We'll make a cut in them to get to the boil."

Charlie was grinning like a crazy possum. He was enjoying all this. That worthless, no-good. . . .

I might have ended up stammering and stuttering for a long time if I hadn't taken a step back and banged my boil into the end of the trestle table. Stars exploded in my head. A searing pain shot through me from the top of my skull to the tip of my toes. I forgot all about the uneasiness I had felt. I just wanted to get rid of that boil.

But I wasn't about to give up any of my dignity by shedding my britches. "I'm not taking off my trousers. I'll . . . ah, I'll drop 'em to my knees, but that's it." I guess all of us grasp for what little dignity we can when we realize we're about to lose it all. Truth is, a jasper can't hold on to much more dignity with his trousers about his knees than about his ankles. But at least, it was a little.

"Fine." Ruth took me by the arm. "Now to the hitching rail."

"To where?" I pulled back.

"The hitching rail," she replied with casual aplomb. "It works better like that."

The panic returned. "What do you mean? I don't understand."

She used her hands to illustrate. "Well, if you're

lying flat, the flesh on your . . . ah, hips is sort of bunched up." She made a bunching gesture with her hands. "It is better if the skin is stretched tight, easier to pull the core out." She led me outside. "Now, come on."

Well, I was mighty glad we were out in the middle of nowhere because I had never been embarrassed so much. Here I was, out in the middle of God and everyone, dropping my trousers to my knees, and leaning over the hitch rail so Ruth could hold my legs and Charlie my arms.

Abruptly, I stood upright. "Are you sure about all this?"

Ruth nodded. "Yes, now bend over."

I did as she said. Now I knew how calves felt at roundup. I watched over my shoulder as Deborah deftly cut my long johns, then touched a match to the blade of her knife and quickly lanced the boil. "Maybe we ought to reconsider this." I tried to pull away, but Charlie and Ruth held me tight.

Ignoring me, Deborah pulled out an empty whiskey bottle. She explained as she carried out the operation. "Paper is rolled into a spindle, set on fire, and dropped into the bottle. I'll place the mouth of the bottle over the boil and as the bottle cools, the core will be sucked out."

I clenched my teeth as the warm bottle touched my skin. Not too bad, I told myself, thinking I had been worried over nothing.

And then the bottle started drawing the core. I stiffened. I couldn't believe it. Sweat popped up on my forehead, soaked my face. That core must have been attached to my toes with wiry little ligaments because I felt like it was going to suck my legs, hips, gun, and all up into that quart-sized whiskey bottle.

My face twisted in agony. I tried to stand upright to relieve the pain, but they held me tight.

Then I felt the core rip loose, and the bottle fell away.

Deborah quickly washed the boil clean, poured whiskey on it, and stuffed cotton into the hole. "That's it. All done."

Shakily, I stood, fumbling to pull my trousers up. The flesh around the boil was still tender, but that would go away.

I looked up at Charlie who was grinning at me. "I could use a drink," I whispered.

Deborah handed me the almost full bottle of whiskey.

I did it justice.

Chapter Fourteen

Physically, Sarah had healed. But, while the wig Ruth and I made a special trip to pick up in Fort Worth covered the scars on Sarah's head, the scars inside refused to heal.

Not once in the next few weeks did she speak. Just the strange humming and unseeing eyes as she sat on the hearth or wandered about the garden with her mother.

Mrs. Winkler still thought I was Harry, her son risen from the grave, but there was one time in front of me when she commented that both her sons were dead. She hesitated, then looked at me in surprise, her eyes animated with a trace of guilt. Suddenly, her eyes went lifeless, and she said. "But you're here, aren't you, Harry?"

Hard to figure.

Ruth was as bright and cheerful as ever. Still there was a coolness between us whenever we were together, a coolness I couldn't explain. Deborah had grudgingly accepted Buckskin Charlie, especially when he put together some of his own stew and whipped up a bowl of spotted pup, a tasty rice and raisin pudding.

Trail herds moved past regularly, forcing us to make more trips to Fort Sill for supplies. From news garnered around the fort, a full scale Indian war was waging in the Texas Panhandle. Federal troops were moving in, trying to run the rebellious warriors back to Indian Territory. In the back of my head, I wondered about Skywalker and Big Tree and the other Indians I had known.

Without my six thousand in gold, I had no reason to head for East Texas, but now that I was healthy, I had no reason to continue to impose on the Winklers. Yet, when I looked around the ranch, I couldn't see how two women could keep it going without hired hands.

I always believed if the water was cold, the best thing was to jump in and get it over with. It's easier to choke down a mouthful of crow when it's warm.

So that night, I made them a proposition.

"You need us and we need you."

We were sitting at the trestle table, the coal oil lamp throwing flickering shadows over our faces.

I continued. "The flood took our money. Blew East

Texas away like a tornado. You have a ranch you need help with if you want it to make a profit."

Ruth glanced at her older sister hopefully.

Deborah's eyes narrowed. A shrewd look wrinkled her forehead. "We got no money to pay hired hands."

"Not now, but you could have. You could build this place into a moneymaking operation. We'll work for keep at first. Then when the ranch starts making money, we can talk pay." I hooked a thumb at Charlie. "You been feeding us the last few weeks. All I'm saying is that we keep the same arrangement, but with something now to work toward."

Ruth spoke up. "I think we should take them up on it. Lord knows we're swamped around here what with the trail herds and stock, not to mention the trouble we've had with Comancheros and Indians."

To my surprise, Deborah agreed.

Our first project was to construct a tower of cottonwood logs at one corner of the cabin. Completely enclosed, the tower was six feet square and rose above the cabin seven feet with gunports near the top and a single entrance from the cabin below. From that vantage point, we had an open field of fire for a mile in any direction, not that I could hit anything at that distance, but maybe at least I could scare someone off.

Next time some jaspers laid siege to the cabin, they couldn't hide in the sage beyond the hardpan.

* * *

Our next trip to Fort Sill, we took the buggy along with the hitch wagon so we could cut down on the number of buying trips, which in turn gave us more time to build the ranch. Among our supplies were additional Winchesters, cartridges, and coal oil, essentials for cowpokes on a cattle drive.

One night after a surprisingly tasty supper, I sauntered outside and leaned up against the hitching rail while I rolled some tobacco. As I touched a match to the cigarette, I wondered just why I was putting so much effort into the ranch, into something that wasn't mine. The only answer I could come up with was that I had nothing better to do.

If I were smart, I'd spend another season with the buffalo, putting together another grubstake. But then, there was the Indian war up in the Panhandle, and I could end up like Sarah with no hair, maybe even dead. Or maybe I should just head on to East Texas and find some means of income there.

I could always drift logs down to Madison or Sabine Pass.

The door opened and Ruth stepped out. She stopped abruptly when she saw me. "Oh," she exclaimed. "You gave me a fright. I didn't see you."

I stepped back. The nervousness I experienced every time I was around her came back. "Mighty fine supper tonight, Miss Ruth."

She flashed a smile. "It was Charlie's recipe."

"Well, it was right good." I had to remember to thank Charlie. In the last weeks, Ruth had been trying more and more of his recipes and fewer of hers.

We stared at the stars for a short while. In the distance, a coyote howled. From behind the barn, an owl hooted.

I felt the coolness between us. For the life of me, I couldn't figure what caused it unless she had been around her sister too long and had taken on a bad temper toward men.

The silence between us grew longer.

"Sarah seems about the same," I said in an effort break the silence.

Her reply was almost inaudible. "Yes. She's no better. I'm afraid that. . . ." Her voice trailed off.

"That she's going to be like Mrs. Winkler?"

Chewing on her bottom lip, she stared at the stars overhead. In a cool, measured voice, she switched the subject. "The ranch looks good, Martin. You and Charlie are doing a fine job."

"Thanks. This place has mighty good possibilities. Why with the water from the river, you can grow just about anything you got a mind to."

She switched subjects again. "Why are you here?" She made a sweeping gesture with her hand taking in the ranch. "Why didn't you go on to East Texas instead of hanging around here?"

I stared at her a few moments. "I've asked myself

that same question, Miss Ruth. Maybe it's because the dream I had is gone and for the time being, I figure this is as good a way as any to repay you folks for taking me in." It seemed I should be saying more, but exactly what I wasn't sure.

"But Charlie—maybe Charlie has something to do, someplace to go."

I arched an eyebrow. "Charlie can come and go when he wants. Always has."

She shook her head. "I just don't understand why he stays."

Taking a deep drag on the cigarette, I considered her remark. "Where would Charlie go, Miss Ruth? His home has been taken over by the white man. His buffalo are disappearing, his family is dead. He has nothing. You have this place. You can go off to New York or New Orleans and have somewhere to come back to. But he's got nothing."

She stared across the prairie. Her words grew cooler. "Well, we do appreciate it, and what you're doing here is making things better, but I hate to see you throw your life away here when you could be doing what you want."

I studied her profile. "What about you, Miss Ruth? Have you ever thought about more than this?"

Maybe my words caught her off guard. I'm not certain, but they did seem to upset her. When she replied, her voice was strained. "What do you mean, like this?"

"You know, a family—one of your own."

She looked up at me. Despite the shadows of the night, I caught a glimpse of pain flicker over her face, quickly replaced with a look of grim determination. "I'll have you know I'm perfectly satisfied with the way things are." She whirled about and headed for the door. "And I'll thank you not to interfere." The slamming of the door added an exclamation point to her request.

Mouth gaping, I could only stare at the door.

That night, I did some soul searching, rethinking the obligation I had taken on with the Winklers. True, they had taken me in and healed me. But I had done a heap of mending and repairing about the ranch. That, with the regular trips to Fort Sill, should be more than enough payback.

So what was holding me?

I didn't know. All I did know was that I wasn't ready to leave.

Nature has a strange way of playing tricks on a body. About the time a jasper figures he has a pat hand, she slips a joker in the deck.

The next morning, a cloud of dust billowed above the eastern horizon. I forgot about the disagreement between me and Miss Ruth the night before. Quickly, we took refuge in the cabin with Charlie and me climbing into the tower.

After some time, dark figures emerged from the dust.

"Looks like cavalry to me," I muttered, peering through the gunport.

Charlie grunted, but we remained in the tower until we were absolutely certain.

Ten minutes later, they reined up.

A colonel saluted us smartly. "Good morning. Colonel Randall MacKenzie at your service."

We invited him in for coffee, but he declined. "We're heading for the Prairie Dog Town branch of the Red River."

I pointed west. "The *Keche-ah-que-ho-no* is what the Kiowa and Comanche call it. Leads up to Palo Duro Canyon. Four or five days from here."

Deborah stepped forward, pausing at Buckskin Charlie's side. She shoved her hat to the back of her head and waved her hand at the mounted troops. "You think you're going to run down them heathen redskins with this collection of bluebellies, soldier boy?"

If he were surprised by her sarcasm or her appearance, he didn't show it. "Yes, ma'am. We hear there's a camp in that Palo Duro Canyon. We're to run the Kiowa and Comanche back to the Indian territory."

"We'd be better off if they was all dead," she spat out.

MacKenzie frowned. I saw his gaze slide from Deborah to Charlie and back. His confusion was obvious.

I spoke up. "We'd be pleased if you'd care to camp here tonight."

He shoved aside his confusion. "I'm obliged, but I have my orders." He peered across the prairie. "Any hostiles in the area?"

"Not that we've spotted. Some dust back to the west from time to time, but none have come by here."

He considered my words. "Surprising. Isolated like you are."

"Not really, Colonel," Ruth said, stepping forward. "We're on the Chisholm Trail here. Every third or fourth day, a cattle drive comes through."

"And Wallace here is friends with some of them Kiowa braves," Deborah put in.

MacKenzie frowned at me. "Friends?"

"I wouldn't say friends. I know some of them. Big Tree was by here a few weeks ago. Hasn't been here since."

"Big Tree? He's one of them we got orders to catch and hang." His suspicious eyes quickly swept the prairie as if hostile Kiowa were hiding in the sage.

I glanced at Charlie. "Hang? Just for leaving the reservation?"

"No. Massacred some bullwhackers down by Jacksboro. Tied them upside down to wagon wheels and built fires under their skulls."

Beside me, Ruth gasped. Deborah's face grew even more grim.

MacKenzie continued. "Can't predict them. Story

we got was that they let a wagon and a patrol of soldiers pass unharmed. It was a good thing. The passenger in the wagon was General Sherman."

Sherman! I shook my head. The entire countryside would have exploded if it had been Sherman tied to that wagon wheel.

We watched as the troops rode off to the west. Far beyond, dark clouds gathered on the horizon. From time to time, lightning streaked through the clouds, jabbing at the ground.

After listening to MacKenzie, the questions I had been tussling with about staying were now shoved from my head. With the troops coming in, the rebel Indians would scatter. No telling where they would go.

And as he said, we were isolated. We couldn't depend on help from the cattle drives. Chances were, once word reached South Texas about the Indian trouble, the drives would shut down.

Throughout the day, the storm clouds grew closer. Even before they reached us, great, fat drops of rain began falling, slowly at first, but as the clouds moved past, faster until the sheeting rain obliterated the river north of us.

Throughout the night, the rain pounded the roof. It was a cold rain, portending of the coming winter, I guessed. The fire in the hearth took away the chill, and that evening, we sat to a supper of fried steak and red-eye gravy and hot biscuits.

Miss Ruth used Charlie's recipe for steak and gravy, and the meal was right tasty except for the biscuits.

One bite into the biscuits, and I knew Charlie was going to have to give her his recipe. The most complimentary remark I could pay them was they would serve just as well as lead in a bullet mold.

But Mrs. Winkler, in an unusual outburst, dropped her biscuit back in her plate. She stopped rocking and stared directly at the fire in the hearth. "I can't eat this biscuit. It's like a rock. What did you do?"

Miss Ruth's face colored. She shot me a sidelong glance. "Nothing, Ma. Just like always. Besides, Martin and Charlie are eating them and not complaining. Why do you always have to. . . ." She hesitated, clamping her lips shut. I could tell from the expression on her face that she was struggling to contain the flush of anger that had swept over her. I wondered then why she didn't just up and say what was on her mind.

Sitting on the hearth, Sarah brushed her hair and hummed that little collection of nameless tunes. Deborah continued her meal, ignoring the sudden tension filling the room. For some reason, I had the feeling this was not an uncommon disagreement although it was the first time I had been witness to it.

Miss Ruth turned to me, her eyes blazing. "Are the biscuits too hard for you, Mister Wallace?" There was a hint of warning in her tone.

"Huh?" I glanced at my plate where I had heaped generous helping of gravy over my biscuits, soaking them. "Why, no, ma'am. They're just fine. How about you, Charlie?"

He grunted and took another bite of gravy and biscuit.

Mrs. Winkler folded her arms over her chest and continued staring at the fire. "Well, I know what I know, and I say they're hard as rocks."

An uneasy silence fell over the cabin.

Outside, the rain pounded on the roof.

After a few moments, Ruth silently rose and retrieved her Ma's plate. In a soft, placating tone, she said. "You want me to fix you something else, Ma? Mush? Or stew?"

Mrs. Winkler shook her head. "Not hungry."

Later, as Charlie and me lay on our soogans out in the barn, I tried to figure out the Winkler family. Of the four, Sarah was the only one I could understand, and that was because her problems were obvious. The scalping had left her touched in the head, probably until her dying day.

Sometimes, I wondered about Mrs. Winkler. Usually, she was in a world of her own, but from time to time, she came out of that world and appeared perfectly normal. Though I felt guilty, sometimes I had the feeling she was a heap smarter than she wanted us to believe.

Miss Ruth seemed to always be kowtowing to her ma, even more than an offspring honoring her parents.

It didn't make sense, but then Deborah didn't make sense either for she was just the opposite. She seldom said a word to her ma, and when she did, it was hostile.

They were a peculiar family, mighty peculiar.

The rain drummed against the barn roof. I rolled over and pulled my blanket about my neck. Maybe I should pack up and leave. My life would be a lot simpler.

Chapter Fifteen

For two more days, the rain continued. The river rose from its banks, a red flood of churning water almost a half mile wide. On the third night, the rain faded into a drizzle. With the drizzle came another sound, one I couldn't put my finger on until I climbed into the barn loft next morning and peered toward the river.

Then I realized what I was hearing, or to be more accurate, what I wasn't hearing. The flood had cut a new river channel farther north about a quarter mile or so.

From my vantage point, I could see a mile or so upriver to where Buckskin Charlie and I had attempted to cross some months earlier, when we were both caught up in the flood.

At that point, the new channel cut back north in a semi-circle through the sandy bank, coming back into the original channel some half-mile downriver from us.

Debris littered the old bed, limbs, branches, and entire trees, all forced downriver by the power of the raging water, now stranded by the shift of the river.

The drizzle continued, a slow, aggravating fall, not so hard as to prevent a jasper from doing his chores, but steady enough to make the task uncomfortable and dull a man's senses.

Mid-afternoon, I grained the ponies while Charlie lugged firewood inside. I'd had a bellyful of the rain, and still it continued to fall.

I shivered, more because I was soaked through and through than because of a chill. I was more concerned with my own comfort than safety, and that was a serious mistake that could have had bad consequences.

Ducking my head between my shoulders and tugging my hat down over my ears, I pushed open the barn door and stepped outside.

Without warning, the heavy door slammed back against my outstretched arm, knocking me back into the barn. At the same time, a portion of the door seemed to explode, followed by the boom of a heavy rifle.

I rolled backward when I hit the ground, shucking my six-gun at the same time. I scrabbled to my feet and rushed to a shuttered window and peered through the cracks.

All I could see was the slow drizzle soaking the prairie. The sage drooped under the weight of the water. I scanned the countryside.

Nothing.

Moving quickly, I hurried from wall to wall, peering through the cracks at the prairie around us. I saw nothing.

The hole in the door was the size of a double eagle. No small caliber Winchester made that. A buffalo rifle, likely.

Tentatively, I eased the door open, remaining out of sight.

A shrill whistle caught my attention.

Charlie waggled the muzzle of his Sharps from one of the gun ports in the tower. I knew what he wanted. Me to draw fire so he would have a target.

I had two choices. His, or wait. If I waited, soon dark would settle over the countryside. I wasn't any too anxious to sit out here all night by myself just waiting for company.

The muzzle waggled again.

"Hold your horses," I muttered under my breath.

I waved back, flexed my fingers about the butt of my handgun, drew a deep breath, and then leaped outside. I jammed my heel in the mud and threw myself back into the barn as a rifle boomed. A chunk of mud the size of my head exploded at where I would have been had I not leaped back inside. I jumped back to my feet and raced for the cabin as Charlie's Sharps roared.

Sloshing through mud and firing a six-gun at the same time doesn't promote any kind of accuracy, but I was hoping the noise and commotion would cause whoever was out there to keep his head down.

There was more than one "whoever" out there, for immediately two rifles spat out lead slugs at me as I stumbled and slid through the muck to the cabin. One slug clipped the toe of my boot. Another hummed past my ear, and a third burned my thigh.

I eyed the heavy cabin door apprehensively, knowing I would have to pause to yank it open. Overhead the Sharps boomed, and out in the prairie, a buffalo rifle roared. I clenched my teeth for the impact. The lead ball slammed into the cabin only inches in front of me.

Just as I reached the door, it opened. I leaped inside and hit the floor rolling as the door slammed behind me.

Ruth stood with her back to the door while Deborah peered through a gun port near the door. Sarah and her Ma sat by the fire, Sarah on the hearth, Mrs. Winkler in the rocker, her eyes glued to a gun port.

Stumbling to my feet, I reloaded, then reached for a Winchester and clambered up into the tower.

"Spot anyone?"

Charlie kept searching the prairie. "Injun. Maybe six. In gully."

"Kiowa?"

He shrugged.

Whatever tribe, they were sly, but then, I can't remember meeting a true warrior who wasn't. From the tower, there were only a handful of spots on the prairie we couldn't see, and those were the ones in which they had chosen to hide.

"You figure they'll try to come in tonight?"

Charlie shrugged again. "I would. Burn barn, then cabin." He spoke so matter-of-factly that I was surprised.

"Burn? But the rain? Everything is too wet."

He finally looked at me. The darkness was growing, but I could see amused disdain in his eyes at my ignorance.

"What?"

"Coal oil."

I gaped at him. Coal oil. I'd forgotten all about our supply stored in the barn. If that raiding party got its hands on the coal oil, it could burn us to the ground. I blew noisily through my lips. "Blast! Looks like we don't have much of a choice, huh?"

Leaving Deborah and Miss Ruth armed with Winchesters and orders to open up for no one, I promised them that if we heard gunfire, we'd hustle back.

Then Charlie and me blew out the lanterns in the cabin and slipped out a rear window. Staying on our bellies, we slithered in the mud and sand through the sage to the corral behind the barn.

By now, darkness covered the prairie. We paused shoulder-to-shoulder, still on our stomachs, peering just over the bottom rail of the corral.

"They might already be inside," I whispered.

"Yep."

"They could be waiting for us."

"Yep."

"Maybe we should split up."

"Yep."

I hesitated. "Don't you have anything to say?"

He grunted. "White man say enough. We go."

Charlie slipped in through the rear door while I sneaked in through the stalls. The ponies recognized my smell and stamped nervously only a few times before turning back to their grain.

Just beyond the stalls, I lay motionless, listening.

The barn was as dark as the inside of a cow. I eased back into a corner, but then moved to my right a few feet and squatted against the ladder to the loft. I visualized the layout of the barn before me.

Forward and to the left were the stalls. Directly ahead was the front door, and back to my right and behind me, the rear. The loft was above, but I didn't figure on anyone coming down from there.

My heart thudded in my chest. I wondered where Charlie had forted up in the barn.

Time dragged. The patter of drizzle on the roof was

mesmerizing. Off to one side, water dripped into a small puddle on the dirt floor, each splash sounding like a gunshot.

Maybe an hour had passed when the ponies nickered nervously. Then I heard the first sound, a soft popping of a foot being pulled from mud. Back in the stalls.

Crooking my thumb over the hammer, I waited until the next time the ponies nickered, and then I cocked it.

I couldn't see my hand right in front of my eyes, but in my mind, I followed the rustle of feet as their owner stepped from the stalls and made his way toward the far wall where we maintained our store of goods and supplies for the wagon trains.

Slowly, I brought my Winchester to my shoulder. I don't care how keen an Indian's senses, he can't see in the dark. He had to have light, and the moment he made some, he was fair game.

Overhead, the loft squeaked. I froze, my finger touching the trigger. My mind raced. Was it just the barn itself, or was someone up there? For several seconds, the drizzle pattering against the roof was the only sound.

I relaxed, and then the loft squeaked again. This time, a few wispy stems of hay drifted down, one settling on my trigger hand.

I held my breath. Had he been up there all along?

He had to have been, so he probably knew Charlie and I were inside also.

The ladder against which I leaned had been nailed to a supporting post, and when the unseen jasper above stepped on the top rung, I could feel the slight movement of the ladder.

I cursed myself for leaving the dark corner to begin with. If I moved now, he would hear me. And if I didn't move, in ten seconds, he was going to be using my shoulders as a ladder rung.

Despite the desperate situation in which I suddenly found myself, I couldn't help chiding myself for always being in the wrong spot at the wrong time.

My pa was never much of a gambler, and he always told me that there was only one sure thing about luck. Sooner or later, it would change.

Well, mine did—right at that second.

The scratching of metal against granite cut through the patter of the drizzle, and a few tiny sparks lit the darkness.

Instantly reacting, I fired twice, one right on top of the other and threw myself aside, chambering another cartridge and firing at the ladder in the darkness above.

In that fraction of a second that my muzzle blast lit the darkness, I glimpsed a surprised face staring down at me from the ladder. Indian. I couldn't tell what tribe, but I did see the jacket he was wearing, an army issue four-button sack coat.

The barn exploded with gunfire. Muzzle blasts

spewed orange bursts, lighting the barn and casting shadows in eerie relief into the corners. I continued rolling, pumping off three more shots before I banged into a support post. At the same time, I listened for gunfire from the cabin. There was none.

A lead slug slammed into the post above my head. Splinters peppered my cheek. I scrabbled around the post and tried to dig a hole in the ground. The acrid odor of burning gunpowder filled the air.

As abruptly as the firing began, it stopped.

For several seconds, tense silence filled the barn, then back to my left, hurried feet sloshed through the mud in the corral. Across the barn, the front door squeaked, then banged shut. I grinned. I held my fire.

A soft whisper came through the darkness. "Wallace?"

"I'm here."

Moments later, a match flared and Charlie stood in its flickering glow. I lit a lantern and held it over my head, expecting to see a couple figures sprawled on the floor.

There was no one. I knelt by the stack of supplies. A few drops of blood were spattered about, a few more by the ladder. "Well, maybe we spooked them enough so they'll think better about coming back."

I turned back to Charlie and froze. A patch of blood was spreading over the shoulder of his worn buckskin shirt. "Charlie."

He had laid his Sharps on the bags of flour and was

gingerly inspecting his wound. He grunted. "Not bad."
He motioned for me to hold the lantern near one corner of the barn. With one swoop of his arm, he
grabbed a handful of spider webs, which he rolled into
a ball and jammed into the wound. Then he removed
his parfleche bag from around his neck and retrieved
a petal of peyote and popped it in his mouth. "No hit
bone," he said, reaching for his Sharps.

Chapter Sixteen

The women had watched the battle, although they had not been able to see a thing other than one or two muzzle blasts, after which they heard feet splashing through water and mud to the west, but that was all.

To be on the safe side, Charlie and me shared guard duty until morning. By then, the rain had passed and with it, the clouds.

We found several sets of footprints. Although the drizzle had melted the edges, we could still follow them to the gully where they had hidden their ponies.

I climbed to the top of the gully and squinted toward the western horizon. "Renegades from the Nation," I said. "Probably been with Chief Quanah Parker and his boys over to the Panhandle. That could explain how that brave picked up the Union soldier's sack coat."

"You think MacKenzie?"

"Possible. Parker could have jumped the Colonel and his troops anywhere along the river."

Charlie indicated the tracks. "Maybe they hide. Let cavalry pass." He made Indian sign for journeying, a short gesture forward with fingers extended and joined.

The morning sun warmed my shoulders. The day promised to be hot.

I studied the lay of the countryside around us. "Reckon with MacKenzie stirring up trouble with the Comanche and Kiowa in the Panhandle, we best keep a sharp eye out. Maybe the colonel will have the situation settled by winter." I grinned and added. "Good thing we don't have any pressing engagements. Things might get kind of interesting around here before MacKenzie gets all the hostiles back on the reservation."

Charlie grunted. "Parker not go back to reservation. Die first."

A few years earlier when I spent time with the Kiowa, I had the chance to meet the Comanche chief, Quanah Parker. He had come to Big Tree's camp for a peace parley. He was an unusual man.

His mother was a white woman, Cynthia Ann Parker. His pa was Peta Nocoma, a young chief who

gained fame for his many violent raids on white set-
tlements in the territory. While prominent Comanche
warriors customarily took several wives, Peta never
took any wife except Cynthia Ann, a mark of extraor-
dinary devotion and honor for her. They had three
children, Quanah, Pecos, and a daughter, Topsannah.

Quanah seemed to be fairly smart, and wise. So
now, I couldn't agree with Charlie that the Comanche
war chief would fight to the death. From what little I
knew of him, I halfway figured that if he ever reached
the point where the odds were against him, he'd toss
in his cards and see if he could get a new deal.

"Maybe he will and maybe he won't, Charlie. You
can't tell just by looking. Besides, just because a
chicken has wings doesn't mean it can fly." I glanced
at the river and changed the subject. "Looks like all
that rain changed the complexion of things around
here."

We wandered toward the river, noting the broad expanse of sand that had once been river bottom. Within
a year, the ubiquitous sage bush would have the sandy
expanse covered. Three years from now, any sign of
the river's old bed would be erased.

Pools of shallow water marked possible quicksand
beds. We paused at the edge of the old bed and peered
across the river. Several hundred yards upriver, I spotted the crossing Charlie and me had taken that night
we were caught in the flood.

The sun grew warmer, drying the wet sand. Overhead, a buzzard drifted by on the gentle currents created by the rising evaporation from the riverbed.

Without warning, the buzzard banked and began circling. The graceful bird spread its wings and came to a lumbering landing near a small protuberance in the sand a couple hundred yards distant. Graceful as the birds are in the air, they are as ungainly on the ground. Wobbling from side to side, the buzzard crabbed up to the protuberance and grabbed it in its powerful beak.

Squawking in anger, the black bird flapped his wings in an effort to rip away a chunk of the object, but whatever it was refused to give.

For a few seconds, Charlie and I looked on in amusement as the buzzard clawed at the object, then grabbed another mouthful and tried to tear it off.

"Wonder what that old boy has got hold of," I muttered, starting across the expanse of old riverbed, taking care to circle the wet spots.

As we drew closer, the buzzard squawked and back-pedaled, almost falling before it could pound its great wings and lift its ungainly body into the air.

Charlie knelt by the protuberance and scraped away the sand. A boot heel. He chuckled. "Someone go barefoot."

My voice shook in excitement. "Pull it up. Maybe it's mine. I lost them in the flood."

The boot came out of its sandy bed easily. Immediately I recognized the stitching on the boot top. I grabbed it and inspected it in disbelief. "It is mine. Why, I'll be hornswoggled and willow switched. It is one of mine." I glanced around. "I wonder. . . ."

I spotted another bulge some ten or fifteen feet up-river.

Quickly, I dropped to my knees and dug into the sand. My fingers scraped against leather. I froze for a moment, then began digging frantically. Seconds later, I uncovered a metal buckle. I brushed frantically as the wet sand clinging to the buckle. My heart jumped into my throat. I could only croak. "Charlie—Charlie—Charlie."

I tore at the sand.

The saddlebags!

I had discovered my saddlebags and the six thousand in gold coins. I slid my fingers under the flaps of the bags and jerked. The saddlebags burst from the riverbed in a spray of sand.

"I can't believe it. I can't believe it." I blabbered the same words over and over as I fumbled to open the bags. When the flap flew back, I gasped. All I saw was sand.

Charlie grunted. I looked up at him in disbelief. Impossible. The flaps were fastened. The coins couldn't have washed out. I dug into the bag, and to my relief, my fingers touched the coins just beneath the layer of sand washed in by the flow of the river.

I jumped up and grabbed Charlie, and we danced over the riverbed like two berserk Indians.

"Now we go East Texas." He laughed.

"Yeah. Now we can buy that plantation. Why we. . . ." The elation that had lifted me off the ground vanished, and I crashed to earth. I gaped at him. "East Texas?"

He nodded enthusiastically.

I looked back at the cabin, and the grin faded from his face. We couldn't just run off and leave the women, not with Indian trouble simmering in the pot.

If we left, the women's chance of survival was as likely as grass growing around a hog trough. On the other hand, the entire plantation might be sold piece-meal before I made it back. And I would have been satisfied with the house and a section of rich soil. A jasper can do a heap with a square mile of lush earth.

Charlie glanced to the west. "Maybe MacKenzie take Big Tree. Maybe war over."

I arched an eyebrow. "After that war party last night?"

He shrugged. "They head north, across river. Maybe we last ones before they go back to reservation."

"That's a mighty big heap of 'maybes'. And maybe you're wrong. You think of that?"

He shrugged again. "Maybe."

I slung the saddlebags over my shoulder, and we headed back to the cabin. For a few seconds, I found myself half wishing I hadn't found the coins because now I was facing a tough decision.

Deborah greeted my discovery of the gold coins

with an arch of a skeptical eyebrow and the remark, "So you was telling the truth after all."

I expected that sort of response from her, but Miss Ruth surprised me for she didn't seem any too excited. I had the feeling she would have been more tickled if I'd brought in a mess of catfish.

Later, as I sat in the shade on the porch and smoked a cigarette, I tried to come up with a plan that would allow me a trip to East Texas to buy the plantation and at the same time, make sure the ranch was well protected. But every idea I came up with had a flaw, forcing me to discard it.

And I might have continued making and discarding plans had not the cavalry patrol ridden in that evening and spent the night in the barn.

Lieutenant Olin W. Brazell took supper with us that evening while his men sat around a campfire and devoured the pot of stew Miss Ruth prepared using one of Charlie's recipes. They were hungry soldiers, tired of their own cooking, and grateful for a woman's meal. And to her credit, the meal was tasty.

Brazell was a bright, perceptive young officer with a ready smile and pleasant demeanor. He quickly sized up our situation within fifteen seconds of entering the cabin. Mrs. Winkler and Sarah sat by the fireplace, one knitting her sweater, the other humming to no one.

Deborah seemed indifferent; Miss Ruth, as always, anxious to make her guest comfortable.

During the meal, Lieutenant Brazell told us of the battle in Palo Duro Canyon. "MacKenzie rousted the hostiles good. Caught them by surprise. Killed most of their ponies, and sent them all packing on foot. Some small bands did make away with some horses. Those are the ones we're chasing down now."

Charlie and I exchanged looks. I turned to the lieutenant. "Big Tree?"

He hesitated, then replied. "Still loose."

"Skywalker."

"No."

"Sitting Bear?"

"Him neither."

Ruth spoke up. "What about the Johannsons? They have a ranch back west."

The young officer's face grew taut, his eyes cold. "We helped bury the old couple. The son—"

"Wilamon," Ruth said. "His name is Wilamon."

Brazell nodded politely. "Wilamon. He's fine. His wife is having problems." He glanced at Sarah. "She had a breakdown."

I knew exactly what he meant.

"Oh, dear," Ruth exclaimed. "We need to see if we can help."

The lieutenant shot me a warning look. I spoke up. "Sorry, Ma'am. Not just right now. With those hostiles out there, it's too dangerous."

"He's right, Ruth," said Deborah, shucking her six-gun and spinning the cylinder. "We best stick tighter than two coats of paint to this place." She slammed the revolver back into the well-oiled holster.

Outside, Charlie and I accompanied the lieutenant back to his men. He glanced over his shoulder to make sure we were out of hearing of the ladies. "I'm relieved you two are here, Mister Wallace. Those warriors you mentioned, Big Tree, Skywalker, and Sitting Bear are the ringleaders. I didn't want to alarm the women, but those three savages are terrorizing the countryside, swearing they'll die before going back to the reservation."

I pulled out the Bull Durham and built a cigarette. I passed it to the lieutenant, who to my surprise deftly built himself one. "I've known those three for years. They always was contrary."

He unbuttoned the top couple buttons on his jacket. "My orders are to track them down. Either bury them or escort them back to the reservation. Big Tree is to go on trial for the massacre of some wagon drivers."

Taking a deep drag on the cigarette, I blew a stream of smoke into the night air. "I heard about that. Well, Lieutenant, all I can say is that you boys got yourself a tall order, but maybe I can help."

"Oh? How's that?" The campfire cast flickering shadows over the frown on his face.

I tossed my cigarette butt to the hardpan and ground

it under my heel. "Charlie and me fought off a handful of hostiles last night. One was wearing an army jacket. They headed north, across the river. I can put you on their trail in the morning."

Chapter Seventeen

Minutes after false dawn pushed its gray fingers across the sky, Lieutenant Brazell and his patrol moved out on the sign of the war party.

Charlie and me stood watching. I don't know about him, but when that last cavalryman splashed out of the river and disappeared through the willows on the far bank, I suddenly felt mighty alone.

Back in the cabin, we sat at the table for a second cup of coffee, planning our day.

Deborah came out of the bedroom wearing a farmer's rigging, blue overalls around the waist of which she had strapped her sixgun. "I'm halfway surprised to see you was still here," she said as she slid the coffee pot from the coals and filled her cup.

"Why wouldn't I be? We have an agreement."

She hooked her thumb toward the saddlebags on the end of the hearth. "You got your money now. No reason to stay."

Her tone oozed with sarcasm, and that rankled me worse than her words. I might not be much in some folks' eyes, but I always kept my word. And I wasn't about to change. At that moment, I wanted to jam that mocking tone of hers down her throat to prove her wrong. Before I knew it, I replied. "This might come as a surprise, Miss Deborah, but I'm staying because I promised I would stay. No amount of money can change that."

And as fast and simple as that, I'd made my decision. And a sense of relief washed over me. I knew I had made the right one.

I glanced at Miss Ruth, but she had her back to me, tending to her mother.

Deborah shrugged and spooned herself a bowl of corn mush.

We spent the remainder of the day readying the cabin for a siege should it come. We filled the water barrel, stocked foodstuffs, loaded the rifles and made sure we had plenty of cartridges.

In the back of my mind, I kept my fingers crossed that the renegade warriors would remember that the Woman-Who-Talks-to-Rocks lived here and avoid us.

* * *

They didn't.

Just before sundown, a horse appeared on the southern horizon, a black speck against the rolling prairie.

Climbing into the loft, I studied the prairie around us, seeing nothing, yet wondering if we were facing some kind of ruse.

Charlie climbed up beside me. "White man. Hurt."

I squinted, but the horse and rider were too distant for me to discern anything except a blur. As they grew closer, I saw the rider was slumped over the neck of his pony.

"You see anything else?" I scanned the prairie, especially the crests of the hills surrounding the injured rider. We had stumbled into the same trap two years earlier when we rode to the aid of what we thought was an injured cowpoke.

Instead, we found a Comanche in white man's clothes and a band of screaming warriors sweeping over the crest of the nearby hills and bearing down on us.

Swift ponies, a heap of luck, and a herd of buffalo saved us.

So now, we were understandably cautious.

"Let him ride on in."

Charlie grunted agreement.

Ten minutes later, the pony halted, and the rider slid to the ground. A quarter-of-a-mile distant.

We studied the situation. "What do you think?" The downed rider was about the same distance from us as he was from the nearby hills. If there were Indians waiting to jump us, we'd have a fair chance of beating them back to the cabin.

"You go," Charlie said. He patted his Sharps. "I watch. I help if trouble."

I looked around at him quizzically. "Why don't you go? I'll stay here with the Sharps."

His copper-colored face took on a look of disdain. "Charlie not trust Wallace with Sharps." He touched his head. "Not want to lose scalp. Wallace trust Charlie."

He was right, blast it.

As I rode out to the fallen rider, I made up my mind that once we got ourselves out of this mess, I would buy my own Sharps and practice until I could shoot rings around him. Then he could do all the dirty work while I stayed back nice and safe.

I grimaced when I reached the cowpoke. A young man, not yet twenty, he had more holes in him than a trail driver's socks at the end of the trail, and he was leaking blood from all of them. I studied the hills about me once more time before I climbed down.

Charlie waved at me, and I waved back.

I slid off my pony, and put the dying boy back on his horse as gently as I could. I rode beside him, holding him in the saddle.

Miss Ruth made the poor hombre comfortable as possible. All he told us before he died was that he and another scout had been hit by a band of twenty or so renegade Indians. He had been cut off from his partner who headed back to the herd.

Behind us, Mrs. Winkler and Miss Sarah sat by the fire, one knitting, one brushing her wig. Deborah let out a big sigh. "Looks like we got problems coming."

"Looks that way," I replied. "Looks that way."

But the problem that came our way turned out to be the last thing I expected.

We took turns in the tower.

Shadows on the prairie at night play tricks on a jasper and fuel his imagination with phantoms that vanish in the blink of an eye. As fatigue sets in, the darkness conjures up more apparitions and specters.

As a result, we broke the night into two-hour shifts between Deborah, Charlie, and me.

It was on Deborah's shift that the trouble started.

Charlie shook me awake. "Wallace."

I jerked awake. I sat upright as a sense of alarm surged through me. The clock in my body told me I had slept longer than my allotted time. I reached for my Winchester. "What's wrong?"

Across the room, Deborah stood staring at me, her jaw set in defiance.

Charlie indicated the door. "Two sisters. They go."

His words bounced off my thick head. "What?"

He nodded to Deborah. "She sleep. I wake. Two sisters, they go."

I looked at Deborah for an explanation, to help me

understand just what the blazes was going on. She glared at me. "It wasn't my fault. I must have dozed. When the Injun there woke me up, Sarah and Ruth was gone."

"Gone?" I asked a brilliant question. "Where?"

Charlie rolled his eyes.

I waved my hand. "Never mind. I'm still trying to get the sleep out of my head." I headed for the shuttered window and peered through a gunport.

Mrs. Winkler sat in her rocker, sleeping. Gently I awakened her. She smiled brightly when she saw me. "Oh, Harry." She frowned, glanced around. Her smile vanished. "Is something wrong?"

"No, ma'am. I was just wondering if you'd seen Ruth or Sarah."

She looked around the semi-dark room as if she were seeing it for the first time. "No, no. Not since this morning when they helped your father in the garden."

Charlie shook his head.

My brain raced, trying to put together some logical explanation. "Let's check the barn."

All the horses were in the stable. There was no indication of the ladies having been there. Pausing outside the barn door, I stared into the night.

The only explanation I could come up with was that Ruth had followed Sarah. But why had Sarah left? I shook my head. As far as the poor woman was concerned, one reason was as good as the other. She might have had a dream; she might have heard a noise; she might have thought she saw something.

"Let's see if we can pick up some sign." Despite the dim glow cast by the lantern, I saw the obvious skepticism on Charlie's face. "At least around the cabin. It's still damp from the storm."

He grunted, but neither of us said what was foremost in our minds. What if they had wandered into the hands of renegade Indians?

We found their sign just beyond the hardpan and followed it across the sand to the water's edge. While I was studying the possibility of crossing and searching for their sign on the far bank now instead of waiting for morning, we heard splashing downriver.

I started to wave the lantern and shout, but Charlie hissed. I doused the lantern, and we dropped to our knees, peering into the night. "Men come."

Even in the starlight, objects on the sandy riverbed stood out. In the distance, dark objects splashed across the river and onto the bed.

We remained frozen, hoping the riders had not spotted the lantern. They continued in their original direction. They must be blind, I told myself.

He nudged me. "We go, now."

Staying in a crouch, we scurried across the bed and into the sage where we could move easier.

We waited in the dark shadows of the cabin as the riders moved past, still heading south. I glanced toward the grave in which we had buried the young trail driver. Was the war party planning on ambushing the trail herd?

"We tracked Ruth and Sarah to the river. Should be able to pick it up on the far side," I told Deborah as I sipped coffee while sitting at the trestle table later that night.

She nodded. "I'll leave at first light."

I shook my head. "No. I'll go. You stay here with Charlie."

She set her jaw. "They left when I was asleep. Besides, I don't trust a man to bring them back, especially one who isn't family."

The hair on the back of my neck bristled. "I don't remember hearing you say that when I saved your hide from those renegades up in the Indian Territory."

She opened her mouth to respond, but then clamped it shut. There was nothing she could say. I continued. "I don't know what happened to you. It's none of my business, but there are a heap of men out there who mean and do what they say. I know the Indian. I've lived with them. That makes me the smart choice to go."

For several moments, she considered what I had said. Finally, she nodded. "All right."

Chapter Eighteen

Buckskin Charlie didn't try to argue me out of the task. He and I had been through the wars together. We knew each other's mind, anticipated each other's actions, and trusted each other's decisions. I paused outside the cabin on my pony and looked down at him and Deborah. "Don't worry," I told her. "I'll find 'em."

I grinned at Charlie. "Watch your hair."

He nodded imperceptibly. "You too."

Swinging east, I cut the trail of the riders who had passed through the night before. The tracks were unshod, about eight or nine. I turned back to Charlie and pumped my Winchester over my head nine times, then headed for the river.

I found Ruth and Sarah's trail without a problem. A couple raccoons had crossed it as had one or two deer and a rattlesnake. From the river, the two sets of tracks wound up a steep, sandy slope that terminated behind the red sandstone bluffs where the tracks milled about, then headed for a tumble of boulders to the north. Halfway to the boulders, Indian ponies cut the trail, but the ponies continued west.

I studied the Indians' trail, wondering how they managed to overlook Ruth and Sarah's.

From the boulders, the trail led back to the sandstone bluffs where it vanished. From the top of the bluff overlooking the river, I spotted the cabin a mile or so distant. As far as I could see in any direction, nothing was moving. I scanned the sandstone bluffs, the tops of which undulated like red waves.

I searched the area around me. All I found was windblown sand holding partial tracks. Slowly, I moved in that direction, up a swollen crest. I jerked to a halt at the top of the crest.

In front of me, the stone sloped down into a deep, broad cave. I shivered. I hated caves. I hoped they hadn't gone into this one. I scanned the countryside about, hoping to spot Ruth and Sarah, but all I saw were swooping hawks being chased by tiny sparrows.

Dismounting, I eased down inside the cave, pausing to look around in wonder. The cave was twelve to fourteen feet high and at least twenty wide. Peering deep into the cave, I was surprised to see patches of sunlight lighting the sandy floor. Obviously, chimneys cut by draining water over the centuries.

I glanced at my feet and caught my breath. Just in front of me were two sets of tracks. By now, I was familiar enough with Ruth and Sarah's to recognize the footprints as theirs. I cursed to myself. They were in here, and I had to follow despite the closed-in, frightened feelings I had in caves.

All along the Red River, stories were told about the looming red sandstone bluffs that overlooked the river. Runoff water cut through the soft red stone, giving the river its name. The sandstone was pocked with caves, and the caves with bottomless shafts.

Hardly a night passed around a campfire without some cowpoke telling of a luckless jasper entering a cave and never returning.

I studied the tracks in the sand at my feet.

Ground-reining my pony, I headed back into the cave. As far as I could see down the cave, the sun splashed bright patches of light on the sandy floor about every forty or fifty feet, but the darkness between the patches was complete. As far as I knew, there could be shafts forty feet wide between the splashes of light.

A torch. That's what I needed. And I had more than enough material just outside. Sage makes a long burning torch if you don't mind the smell, an acrid, stinging odor that shrivels your nose and stings your eyes.

I built four torches, planning on turning back when

I lit the third one. I figured I had about thirty minutes of searching. If I found something, I could always build more torches and return.

For the first few minutes, I found only their tracks. The cave led down into the interior of the sandstone cliffs. Then I passed beyond the sunlight, into the absolute darkness of the cave.

Abruptly, I jerked to a halt.

Directly in front of me, a great hole covered over half the width of the cave. Chills ran up my spine as I saw two sets of tracks approach the edge of the shaft, and only one set back away and skirt it.

Blood pounded in my ears, filling them with a great roaring that threatened to explode my brain. My breathing grew shallow and rapid. I gasped for breath to still the spinning in my skull.

Even before I sucked in that first gasp, I knew that Ruth was the one who had fallen. Had it been Sarah, I would have met Ruth coming back for help.

I dropped to my belly, eased to the edge of the shaft, and held the flickering torch into the abyss. My heart leaped into my throat.

Ten feet down on a ledge, Ruth lay unconscious.

Far below came the rush of water, and cool air bathed my sweaty face. Frantically, I tried to decide my next move.

A rope! I needed a blasted rope, but what if she awakened before I returned and rolled off the ledge?

I could awaken her before I left, but then I might startle her. Maybe if I called her name softly. . . .

I had two or three choices, and all of them dangerous.

Lighting another torch, I dropped the first one down the shaft. It floated down a few seconds, then hit bottom. Seconds later, the fire went out, but before it did, I saw it move to my left. Water. Moving water. About thirty feet or so below Ruth.

I closed my eyes and said a short prayer. No telling how deep the water, which was not an important point for shallow or deep, there was no way out. A jasper would either drown or starve.

Leaning as far over the edge as I dared, I whispered. "Ruth. Miss Ruth." At first, I thought an eyelid fluttered, but then I chalked it up to the flickering light from the sagebrush torch.

I called again. Still no response. Maybe I would have time to retrieve the rope before she awakened.

At that moment, she moaned.

"Miss Ruth. Don't move. Don't move."

She stirred, then shifted her shoulders.

"Don't move, Ruth. Don't move a muscle."

She blinked once or twice, then stared up at me, her eyes wide with fright. I hurried to calm her. "Take it easy. I'll get you out of here. Just take it easy, and don't make any sudden moves.

She stammered. "Wh . . . Where is Sarah?"

"Don't worry about her. We'll find her. We've got to get you out of there first. Can you sit up?"

"Yes."

"Okay. Now, don't move fast. You're on a narrow ledge. Feel with your right hand, real slow."

Keeping her eyes on mine, she explored with her right hand. When her fingers touched the edge of the narrow shelf on which she lay, a horrified gasp sounded in her throat.

"Stay calm. I'll get a rope and pull you out."

"No. No. Don't leave me."

I looked down at her in frustration. "But the rope."

"No. Don't go." She was on the verge of panic.

"All right. I'll stay." Then I had an idea. Quickly, I removed my gun belt and slipped my six-gun under my waistband. "Here. Grab the belt and stand up. I'll pull you up."

Ruth nodded and tried to grin. "I got it."

"Stay next to the wall. If you slip, you've got to hit the ledge."

"All right."

I laid the burning torch on the ground by my foot and seized the belt with both hands. "Here we go."

Slowly, I started easing her up the side of the shaft.

Without warning, an explosion deafened me, and a powerful force struck the heel of my boot, spinning me around and sending me tumbling into the shaft. I heard Ruth scream, and then I hit the icy water.

I shot to the surface, sputtering and coughing just

as Ruth slammed into the water beside me. I pulled her close to me as she coughed out the water she had swallowed.

Luckily, the water was only chest deep. The bed beneath my feet was hard.

A brightly burning torch appeared in the mouth of the shaft. Skywalker and Sitting Bear squinted down into the darkness. I hoped they wouldn't spot us, but they did.

Skywalker leered. "Now you die, Wallace. Long time, but you die." He pulled his battered Henry to his shoulder, but Sitting Bear stopped him.

"No waste bullet. Wallace dead. He starve."

The cruel idea struck Skywalker as funny. "You and your squaw die, Wallace."

Ruth clutched my arm, and pressed her head against my shoulder. I could feel her tremble.

But Skywalker was wrong about starving. The icy water would kill us first.

And then the torchlight vanished.

I had expected total darkness, but to my surprise, a dim glow of light broke the darkness at the base of the shaft below the water.

Ruth exclaimed. "Martin. Look. There's some light."

"I see it," I answered, excited at the flickering glow. The current at my back eased me toward the light. We couldn't be lucky enough to have fallen in a shaft that opened to the river. I looked around at Ruth. Her face was a faint shadow in the dim glow. "There isn't a lot of light. It's either a long tunnel or a crooked one."

"I don't understand what you mean."

"There isn't much light. If the tunnel was only eight or ten feet long, there would be more light."

"What if it's crooked?"

"It couldn't be too crooked or no light at all could make it in."

"Oh."

"I'll go under and see."

She grabbed my arm. "No. It's too dangerous."

I couldn't resist chuckling.

"Why are you laughing?"

"You think we're not in a dangerous spot now?"

For a moment, she hesitated, then sighed. "Just be careful."

"It'll be simple. I'll just squat down and look into the opening. That's all." I peeled off my vest and shirt and tied them together. "Here. Take one end. I'll hold the other. If the current starts pulling me into the opening, I'll jerk on the shirt. Yank me out."

"Just be careful." Her teeth chattered.

Shivering, I took several deep breaths, more than necessary, but that was because I was trying to gather the nerve to enter the opening.

Finally, I drew my last breath, muttered a short prayer, and plunged under the icy water.

The frigid cold penetrated to the marrow of my

bones. I tried to ignore it as I studied the opening with one hand extended and the other clutching the sleeve of my shirt.

The light grew brighter. The opening appeared about three feet wide and the same high. A few feet inside the mouth of the tunnel, a bright glow lit the shaft, revealing even the reddish color of the sandstone bed over which the water flowed.

I dropped to my knees and crawled a couple feet into the tunnel. The current tugged vigorously at me, but I managed to stick my head around the bend and see the light of day.

The tunnel narrowed to a small opening. We'd have to squeeze out.

That's when the snake swirled past me, drawn outside by the current. I jerked back, banged my head on the rocky roof, and swallowed a gallon of water before I could scrabble back and jump to my feet. I came up coughing and sputtering.

"Martin! Are you all right?" She pounded on my back.

My heard thudded in my chest. A snake! Despite the cold, sweat popped out on my face.

"Are you all right?"

"Yeah, yeah. Fine. Just got choked." I kept quiet about the snake.

"Can we make it out?"

For a moment, all I thought about were snakes. Were we in the middle of a nest? Or had the one simply fallen into the shaft with us. Stammering, I nodded emphatically. "Yeah. Just a few feet." I looked around the darkness of the shaft, then laid my hand on her shoulder. "About two feet into the opening, the tunnel cuts back to the left. Five more feet and we're out. It's a narrow opening. You'll have to squeeze through. I'll be right behind you."

She caught her breath. For a moment, her shoulders trembled under my hand. Then in a soft voice, she whispered. "All right. I'm ready."

I hesitated, wondering if I could squeeze through. I drew another deep breath and counted. "Here we go, then. Ready? One, two, three."

We both submerged. I pushed her ahead of me. We had to bend sharply at the waist to twist around the corner. She slid through the small opening easily. For me, the fit would be tighter. I just hoped a snake didn't try to go through at the same time.

Skin peeled from my shoulders, but I made it through. Moments later, we broke into the sunlight.

Still pushing Ruth ahead of me, I stumbled from the water, searching for the water snake, but it was nowhere to be seen.

We were well hidden in a tumble of red boulders in the middle of the willows lining the bank. We both plopped down on the boulders to rest, and savor our freedom. Ten minutes earlier, our chances wouldn't have been worth a Confederate dollar. Now, we were within sight of the cabin.

But, Skywalker and his band were still around. They might not have even had time to return to their ponies.

"We'll stay in the willows until we're even with the cabin. Then we'll cross."

She shook her head. "But, what about Sarah? We've got to find her."

"We will, but I'll get you back to the cabin first, and then I'll find her."

Reluctantly, Ruth agreed, and slowly we made our way downriver. As we picked our way over the boulders and through the willows, she explained that the preceding night she had awakened to find Sarah gone. She saw her by the river and went after her, finally reaching her when Sarah hid in a tumble of boulders at the top of the bluffs. While they were there, a war party of Indians passed, so the two women remained hidden until morning when Sarah suddenly broke for the sandstone bluffs and disappeared into the cave.

"I went after her and fell into the shaft," Ruth said. "I don't know how long I was unconscious."

I remembered the sign I'd followed. Exactly as she said.

"Hold up," I muttered, laying a hand on her arm and pausing.

The cool, clear water burbled as it rushed past. The sandstone bluffs loomed over us. Before us lay a hundred yard stretch of shallow river and another four hundred yards of sand between the riverbank and us. Overhead, a hawk circled, searching for prey.

I glanced back up at the crest of the bluffs.

We were in the clear.

Taking her hand, I said, "Let's go."

Raising our feet high, we splashed through the water, expecting shouts of alarm at every step. Once or twice, Ruth stumbled, slowing us. I glanced over my shoulder.

No sight of the war party.

By now, we reached the sandy riverbank, and I was beginning to think we might make it after all.

A voice sounded from behind.

I looked back and jerked to a halt.

Sarah stood in the middle of the river with a painted brave astride a war pony racing down the bluff toward her. He waved a menacing spear over his head.

I pushed Ruth toward the cabin. "Go," I yelled, spinning on my heel and sprinting back to Sarah. I reached for my six-gun and grabbed air. That's when I remembered my handgun was at the bottom of the shaft.

Chapter Nineteen

The afternoon sun beat down, but chills ran up and down my spine as I watched the war pony draw closer to Sarah. Without any weapons, I had no idea what I was going to do if I reached her first.

I glimpsed movement on the sandy slope at the top of the bluffs. A second warrior was driving his pony toward the river.

Two of them.

Clenching my teeth, I drove my legs faster. My lungs burned, and I gasped for air. At the same time, I wondered about the other Indians in the war party.

As if by magic, they appeared at the top of the slope.

I couldn't whip them all, but I didn't even consider

turning back. By now, I was within twenty yards of Sarah, yelling at her to run.

In her own little world, she simply walked and hummed, staring at her hands that held nothing.

I shouted. "Sarah! Run, run. Hurry! Behind you."

The warrior was closing fast. And then I recognized him.

Skywalker. His thin lips were twisted in a cruel sneer. He lifted his spear, ready to drive it through her back.

The water grabbed at my feet. It seemed as though I was stumbling through a foot of gumbo mud while the war pony seemed to skim the surface of the river.

Skywalker rose in his stirrups and drew back his arm.

I threw myself through the air at Sarah just as the Kiowa brave released the spear.

My shoulder caught her in the mid-section, doubling her over. The spear missed her by less than a frog's hair split down the middle.

At that moment, gunfire sounded back to the west. Skywalker jerked his pony around and tried to locate the source of the shooting.

That pause gave me enough time to leap to my feet and charge his pony, which reared abruptly, causing the warrior to momentarily lose his balance. While the war pony pawed air, I grabbed Skywalker's foot and shoved, forcing him out of the saddle.

He tumbled backward into the river. I jumped on him faster than a duck on a June bug, grabbing for his knife. He seized my wrist with both hands in a desperate effort to keep me from jerking his knife from its sheath.

We rolled through the water, poking and biting and kicking when we could. There were no Marquis of Queensbury rules here, only survival.

I jammed my head under his chin so he couldn't use his body for leverage. I could hear his strained grunts, and suddenly, a excruciating pain in my neck paralyzed me momentarily.

Then I felt Skywalker's teeth chewing into the back of my neck. The pain sent a shot of adrenaline charging through my veins. I yanked away and ripped the knife from its sheath.

In an instant, the Kiowa warrior was on me, one set of fingers about my throat, forcing my head under water, the other grasping my wrist.

The current forced water up my nostrils, choking me. In a move of desperation, I jammed my heel in the sand at my thigh and with a savage grunt, levered my hips and torso up and to the side, throwing Skywalker off me.

We both leaped to our feet, and he charged, head down, arms extended. I stumbled backward and fell, at the same time bringing my feet up into his belly and sending him tumbling over me.

I staggered to my feet. My lungs burned, my throat

throbbed. I glanced toward the shore. The second war pony was heading for me, but the remainder of the war party was retreating back up the slope.

With spray flying from their remounts' feet, a cavalry patrol burst out of the river and raced up the slope after the fleeting renegades.

Suddenly, an arm like steel clamped around my throat and vise-like fingers seized my wrist.

With my free arm, I slammed my elbow into Skywalker's kidney. He grunted, and I dug my elbow into him again and again. His fingers loosened about my wrist. Abruptly, I grabbed his hair and snapped my torso forward, bending at the waist and flipping the surprised Kiowa over my head.

Skywalker sprawled in the water, his head at my feet.

Instantly, he kicked at me, catching me on the forehead and knocking me backward into the water. I fell across the spear he had thrown at Sarah.

In the next second, Skywalker erupted from the water and leaped at me, arms extended, his claw-like fingers reaching for my throat. I brought the knife up, trying to brace the butt against my belly.

He slammed into me, and suddenly, he stiffened as his fingers reached my throat. His eyes grew wide in shock. He struggled to speak, but the words failed him. Hot blood pouring from his belly covered my thumb and forefinger before the current washed it away. With an effort, I drove the knife deeper in his belly, twisting it at the same time.

The hot smell of offal assailed my nostrils.

Over his shoulder, I spotted the second Kiowa, Sitting Bear, only a few feet distant. Wearing a sneer on his lips, he leaned forward over the neck of his pony, grinning evilly at me. Abruptly, he sat upright in his saddle.

He jerked his Winchester to his shoulder, but a shot rang out from behind me. A geyser of water exploded in front of the war pony. Sitting Bear shifted the muzzle of his rifle from me and fired two quick shots.

That gave me time to roll the dead Skywalker off me and jump to my feet. I grabbed the spear I had been lying on and charged the horse.

Sitting Bear tried to jerk the muzzle of his Winchester down, but I drove the head of the spear beneath and into his chest, knocking him backward over the croup of his pony.

He slammed to the water, grasping frantically at the shaft impaling him. With a savage grunt, I drove the spear through him, pinning him against the river bottom.

I jerked around, searching for whoever had fired the shot that distracted the Kiowa brave.

Beyond the water, on the sand, sprawled Deborah, arms outflung, head thrown back. I rushed to her side. Blood gushed from the side of her neck and from the hole in the middle of her chest. Gently, I raised her head. Her breath rattled in her lungs.

"W . . . Wallace?" The word was barely a croak in the throat.

"Yes. I'm here."

She struggled to open her eyes. Blood ran down the corner of her lips. "Th . . . Thanks."

A cry of pain jerked me around. Ruth was racing across the sand, her brown hair flying out behind her, and her arms flailing the air. She dropped to her knees beside Deborah and hugged her big sister to her breast.

"Deb—Deb, please, don't die. Don't die."

Deborah's eyes opened slightly. She coughed and blood splattered Ruth. "R . . . Ruthie. I . . . I . . ." Ruth leaned closer, and Deborah whispered to her. I heard the faint word, "Harry," and then her voice faded. Moments later, Ruth stiffened, then sobbed and clutched Deborah to her.

I thought I glimpsed a faint smile on Deborah's lips before she died.

Back in the river, Sarah sat waist deep in the current, studying her hands and humming a tune only she knew. I splashed through the water to her. She looked up at me curiously, and I said. "Let's go, Sarah. Your ma is waiting."

"Oh." She nodded. "All right. If you insist." In a ladylike gesture, she offered me her hand. "Mother can be so impatient."

We stopped beside Ruth and Deborah. Ruth looked

up at me, her eyes red, her face revealing her numbed feelings. "I'll carry her back to the cabin," I said, giving her Sarah's hand and gently lifting Deborah and holding her to my chest.

Ruth's eyes brimmed with tears. She spoke in a hoarse whisper. "Thank you, Martin."

There was something different in her tone, something I couldn't put my finger on.

Charlie rode in from the south as we reached the cabin. He dismounted and looked at Deborah, then me. I told him what had happened.

When I mentioned the cavalry patrol, he grunted and pointed the muzzle of his Sharps to the south. "More bluecoats there. Not far." Not far for Charlie usually meant a two or three hour ride. "I see, but not speak."

While building a casket for Deborah, we pondered the implication of so much cavalry in the area. I hoped it was what I thought, but I didn't figure we could be that lucky. Miss Ruth brought us coffee twice. Despite the tragedy she had faced that day, the cool demeanor she had always worn about her had vanished. In its place she exuded nervous warmth and concern.

After a surprisingly tasty supper that night, she came outside to stand beside me while I smoked a cigarette. She cleared her throat. "Mister Wallace, I think I need to apologize for how I've acted at times over the last few months."

"No need." I shrugged, puzzled by her words. Sure, she'd been distant and cool at times, but I attributed that to her being a woman and tried to think nothing else about it.

Reluctantly, she explained. "You see, I blamed myself for Harry's death. Oh, I told him about the Indian trouble, but he went anyway." Her brows knit as the memories came back. "Harry was the youngest, Ma's favorite. She was crushed. I told myself I should have tried harder, but I was too selfish. You see, there was a brush arbor revival at the Shoop ranch that night, and I was more interested in what I would wear so I didn't take the extra time to talk him out of it.

She hesitated and gave me a wan smile. "Turns out that Deborah saw him later. She told him I was just being too cautious, that there had been no Indians for weeks." She paused, then hastily added. "And she was right. There hadn't been."

"So when Harry was killed, she kept quiet so your ma wouldn't blame her, is that it?"

Ruth winced. "It sounds hard to put it like that."

I shrugged. "Maybe so, but it's the truth. That's what she was whispering to you back at the river?"

"Yes."

"And that's why you always paid your ma so much attention?"

"I felt guilty." She looked up at me.

My breath came fast. Before I could think, I leaned down and kissed her lightly. "Now you know."

She smiled brightly, and even in the starlight, I could see her eyes glittering with excitement. "Now I know."

We buried Deborah next morning, and as Charlie and me packed the last soil on her grave, the thundering of pounding hooves echoed across the prairie from the west.

Quickly retreating to the front of the cabin, we watched as the riders emerged above the sage. Indians! A war party of Comanche and Kiowa. "Inside," I ordered, slamming the door behind me and following Charlie into the tower.

Led by Black Coyote, the small party of eight slid to a halt in front of the cabin. Black Coyote's left arm hung limply at his side, a bloody bandage around the bicep. He looked up at the tower. "Wallace?"

I slid the barrel of the Winchester through the gunport. "I'm here."

"I not make war."

I studied the other warriors. They wore the look of defeat. "What do you want here?"

"Bluecoats follow. We go to reservation. There we stay with Skywalker and Sitting Bear."

"Not with them, you won't, Black Coyote. They're out there in the river, feeding the fish."

For the first time in the ten years I had known Black

Coyote, the impassive expression on his face cracked. He knit his brows as he glanced at the river. He shrugged. "It is of no matter. We return to reservation."

"For more war?"

He gazed longingly at the prairie surrounding us. "There will be no more war, Wallace. The red man is no longer a man." For several moments, he stared up at me.

I pulled the Winchester from the gunport and stared down at Black Coyote. To my surprise, I felt sorry for him, and those riding with him. A way of life was forever gone. "Take care," I said. "Take care."

Our eyes met. He nodded, and pulled his pony around.

I watched from the tower until the small band disappeared over the sandy slope beyond the river.

I looked at Charlie. Were the Indian wars over after all these years, really over? It was hard to believe that the Comanche and Kiowa were returning to the reservation.

Ten minutes later, three patrols of cavalry rode through, stopping long enough to inform us that the last of the renegades had been forced back to the reservation.

I looked at Ruth. She smiled back.

The wars were over.

That evening a rider came in from a trail herd due to hit the Red in a couple days. He left a list of supplies they would need. Later while Charlie and me were feeding the stock and readying the supplies for the herd, he brought up the question that had been foremost in my mind all afternoon.

"Well, Wallace. What you plan? Bronco Indians back on reservation. You got gold eagles back. You go to East Texas now?"

There it was, the question I had been avoiding for a reason I was afraid to voice. "Haven't decided," I replied, crawfishing. "Maybe later."

But, I couldn't avoid the question. Ruth brought it up that night at the supper table.

She had whipped up a pot of stew, this time using Charlie's recipe. It was right tasty, and the six-shooter coffee was hot and strong. Sarah sat at the table with us, toying with her stew. Mrs. Winkler sat in front of the fireplace, tending to her knitting.

After supper, I paused beside Mrs. Winkler to roll a cigarette. I snapped off a dry branch from a log and touched it to the flames. As I waited for it to catch, Ruth asked. "Now that the Indians are back on the reservation, are you and Charlie moving on to East Texas?"

I hesitated, then touched the burning twig to my cigarette.

Mrs. Winkler paused in her knitting. She looked up at me with bright, animated eyes as she spoke to Ruth.

"No, dear. I haven't finished Mister Wallace's sweater. Besides, he's put too much work in the ranch to leave it now." She smiled sweetly at me and went back to her knitting.

For several seconds, we all just stared at her. I gave Ruth a puzzled frown. "Did she say what I thought she said? Did she call me Wallace?"

I glanced back at the old lady. She looked up at me and winked, then went back to her business of knitting me a sweater.

Ruth was watching me breathlessly. Charlie was helping himself to another bowl of stew. My heart thudded against my chest loud enough, I thought, for everyone to hear.

My cheeks burned. I cleared my throat. "Well, I have done a heap of work, and I would hate to see it fall apart. Besides, that six thousand dollars would go a long ways to helping us build a right respectable spread here."

The beaming smile that leaped to Miss Ruth's lips gave me my answer.

I glanced at Mrs. Winkler, studying her several seconds. Maybe she wasn't as crazy as I thought. Maybe she wasn't crazy at all.

She paused and arched an eyebrow at us. "But you two going to have to get married first. I ain't having no sin in my house."

Charlie chuckled. He pushed himself from the table. "Night, boss. I'm heading for the barn."

"Hold on," I said. "I'm going with you." I leaned forward and kissed Ruth and grinned at her Ma. "We don't want no sinning in this cabin. Not yet."